THE

STAR TREK®

CRAFT BOOK

THE

STAR TREK®
CRAFT BOOK

ANGIE PEDERSEN

GALLERY BOOKS

New York London Toronto Sydney New Delhi

Gallery Books
A Division of Simon & Schuster, Inc.
1230 Avenue of the Americas
New York, NY 10020

For information about special discounts for bulk purchases, please contact Simon & Schuster Special Sales at 1-800-456-6798 or business@simonandschuster.com

Printed in the United States by RR Donnelley.

10 9 8 7 6 5 4 3 2 1

Library of Congress Cataloging-in-Publication Data available upon request.

ISBN: 978-1-4767-1864-4

The Star Trek Craft Book is produced by becker&mayer!, Bellevue, Washington.
www.beckermayer.com

Editor: Leah Jenness
Designer: Katie Benezra
Photo researcher: Kara Stokes
Production coordinator: Diane Ross
Managing editor: Michael del Rosario
Photographer: Jessica Eskelsen
Hand model: Emily Zach

Page 2: Spock and Kirk in the first season of The Original Series.

CONTENTS

Kirk, Uhura, McCoy, and Scott await their transport back to the ship before a transporter malfunction sends them into the Mirror Universe in "Mirror, Mirror" (*TOS*).

INTRODUCTION

S tar Trek, in all its variations, has endeared itself to me, as it is a thread woven throughout my life. Some of my earliest elementary school memories involve *Star Trek*. My brother and I used to eat dinner on little folding trays while watching Kirk battle some unimaginably fierce alien or charm a hazy woman in a gauzy dress. I remember seeing *Star Trek II: The Wrath of Khan* in the theater with my dad. He was so excited to see such a grand villain on the big screen, and the fifth-grade me was mesmerized as my dad described the backstory of the *S.S. Botany Bay* and its inhabitants.

When I met my husband in college and learned of his passion for the show, I knew I'd found a keeper. Together we've raised our children with a healthy appreciation for all things *Trek*, guiding them through each series, episode by episode (including the animated series), and attending the midnight showing of each new movie.

Throughout it all, I've come to appreciate and respect the pioneering elements of the series, how it tested the boundaries of social mores and how it has inspired generations of viewers "to boldly go where no one has gone before."

That's just what we want to do with this book. While full of geeky goodness and just plain fun to make, each project pays homage to the quintessential essence of *Star Trek*—the encouragement to seek out new experiences and embrace the spirit of adventure.

May each project speak to that part of you that longs to explore strange new worlds and imagine the unimaginable. Use this book to try new crafting techniques and materials—you'll find everything from crochet to decoupage, from fleece to fun fur. We've also included a chapter on hosting a theme party so you can gather with your fellow fans in *Star Trek* style.

As a bonus, each project includes tidbits of *Star Trek* lore, giving you a closer look at characters and backstories to lend more meaning to your crafting.

Whether you're a "Trekker in Training" or a seasoned craft whiz, you'll find a project in these pages that piques your interest. Have fun exploring! May you live long and prosper.

The *U.S.S. Enterprise* NCC-1701 circling a Class K planet in "I, Mudd" (*TOS*).

HOW TO USE THIS BOOK

This book is broken down into five sections with five crafts apiece, which makes it easy to work your way through the book project by project or to skip around according to your crafting whimsy. In each section you'll find a list of supplies, step-by-step instructions for completing the craft, helpful photos, and insightful tips for making each project easier.

We've also included a craft Starfleet ranking from Ensign to Admiral to indicate the level of time and difficulty of each project.

· **Ensign:** Perfect for the beginner, projects with this ranking will introduce you to the crafting Starfleet Academy. They're quick and easy.

· **Captain:** Designed for those with intermediate crafting experience, projects with this ranking will help demonstrate your crafting leadership skills. These projects require some skill and time.

· **Admiral:** At the top of the crafting hierarchy, projects with this ranking will test your mettle in crafting battle. These projects are the most complicated and time-consuming in the book. Perfect for when you're in the mood for a crafting challenge!

We've also included a glossary that defines all the crafting terms used in this book. Defined terms are set bold on first reference in the text.

Finally, be sure to check out the appendix, where you'll find all the patterns you need to complete every project. You'll need to enlarge some patterns to fit the project specifications— you can do that on a copier or by scanning the pattern into your computer and manipulating it with a graphic editing program, such as Adobe Photoshop. We've included sizing recommendations when appropriate.

STAR TREK SERIES ABBREVIATIONS

TOS
Star Trek: The Original Series (1966–1969)

TAS
Star Trek: The Animated Series (1973–1974)

TNG
Star Trek: The Next Generation (1987–1994)

DS9
Star Trek: Deep Space Nine (1993–1999)

VOY
Star Trek: Voyager (1995–2001)

ENT

TOOLS & SUPPLIES

The following lists of suggested tools and supplies will get you crafting at warp speed. While we provide a list of materials needed for each project, feel free to substitute however your spirit of adventure dictates. You should be able to find everything you need at a local craft store, but venture into new frontiers like thrift stores and dollar stores to find crafty materials, too.

TOOLS

- Craft blade
- Crochet hooks: F, G, L
- Drill and drill bit
- Fabric-marking tool
- Glue gun
- Graphic editing software, like Adobe Photoshop
- Heated stencil-cutting tool
- Jewelry pliers
- Iron
- Paintbrushes: bristle and foam
- Paper punches: circle
- Printer or photocopier
- Rotary cutter (optional)
- Ruler or tape measure
- Scissors
- Sewing machine
- Tapestry needle
- Teflon presser foot (optional)
- X-acto knife

SUPPLIES

- Acrylic paint
- Acrylic sealant (optional)
- Adhesive foam
- Beads
- Bells or other noisemakers
- Binder clips
- Brads
- Butcher paper
- Buttons
- Canvas sneakers, plain
- Cardstock
- Ceramic tile
- Chipboard book
- Chipboard/cardboard box: circular, with lid
- Chipboard letters
- Cookie sheet
- Cording
- Cork
- Craft glue
- Crochet thread
- Cutting board
- Decoupage glue, such as Mod Podge
- Dowel
- D rings
- Dritz Fray Check (optional)
- Elastic
- Embroidery supplies: hoop, floss, needle
- Enamel craft paint
- Eyelets and eyelet punch
- Fabric: cotton/broadcloth, fleece, gold lamé, metallic, poly-cotton blend, quilted, satin, toweling
- Fabric glue
- Fabric marker
- Faux fur
- Felt

- Fiberfill
- Foam
- Freezer paper
- Fusible web, such as Heat'n Bond
- Glass and bead glue
- Glass cube
- Glue sticks
- Googly eyes
- Guitar picks with predrilled holes
- Holographic spandex
- Iron-on interfacing
- Iron-on transfer paper
- Jewelry-making supplies: jump rings or wire
- Lollipop or cake pop sticks
- Marabou trim
- Masking tape
- Mini lights
- Newsprint (optional)
- Nylon webbing
- Paper
- Paper towels
- Patterned paper or paper with a metallic finish, such as some scrapbooking paper
- Pegboard
- Pencil
- Permanent markers
- Pillow form
- Pinewood plaque

- Polymer clay
- Ribbon
- Scrapbooking paper
- Screen mesh
- Serving platter/charger
- Sewing supplies: needles, threads, and pins
- Sew-on hook and loop tape
- Silk-screen ink
- Socks with colored heel, calf-length
- Spray paint
- Stencil adhesive
- Stitch marker (optional)
- Stretched canvas
- Studs
- Tailor's marking chalk (optional)
- Template plastic
- Toothpicks
- Wax paper
- Wineglass charm hoops
- Velcro
- Vinyl
- Wood men/game pieces
- Yarn
- Zipper

Uhura checks in on a communication channel in "What Little Girls Are Made Of" (*TOS*).

1

THE DÉCOR EFFECT

1: "GO BOLDLY" CANVAS

2: "INFINITE DIVERSITY IN
INFINITE COMBINATIONS"
ENVELOPE-STYLE PILLOWCASE

3: CAPTAIN JAMES T. KIRK
STYLIZED FUSE BEAD FORM

4: *STAR TREK:
THE ANIMATED
SERIES* COASTERS

5: *U.S.S. ENTERPRISE* GLASS
BLOCK DECORATION

I F YOU CAN'T TURN YOUR LIVING ROOM INTO A LIFE-SIZE REPLICA OF THE *U.S.S. Enterprise* BRIDGE, AND A WORKING HOLODECK JUST ISN'T IN THE BUDGET, TURN TO THESE PROJECTS TO SPICE UP YOUR DÉCOR IN *Star Trek* STYLE.

Since we first heard the words "Space: the final frontier" in the opening of *TOS* in 1966, the *U.S.S. Enterprise* and her crew have come across many "new civilizations" in their voyages. First contact with alien races—some friendly, some not nearly so—proved enlightening and sometimes paradigm shifting.

In the inaugural two-part episode of *TNG*, "Encounter at Farpoint," Captain Jean-Luc Picard and his crew first meet Q, an arrogant omnipotent being who puts the human race on trial as "barbarians," charging Picard with its defense.

Picard solves the mystery of Farpoint Station, securing a victory for humankind in Q's challenge and the right to continue exploring the vast unknown of space. "The unknown is what brings us out here," Picard says.

This wall canvas will remind you to face challenges with the courage and fortitude of your favorite explorers. Use Picard's Starfleet uniform color as your background, or choose a color to suit your own décor.

Space: the final frontier. These are the voyages of the Starship Enterprise. Its five-year mission: to explore strange new worlds, to seek out new life and new civilizations, to boldly go where no one has gone before.

"GO BOLDLY" CANVAS

BY ANGIE PEDERSEN

TOOLS & SUPPLIES

- 8-INCH × 16-INCH STRETCHED CANVAS
- ACRYLIC PAINT (DARK RED/ MAROON FOR PICARD'S UNIFORM)
- 1-INCH PAINTBRUSH
- PENCIL
- 1 PIECE PATTERNED SCRAPBOOKING PAPER, SILVER
- SCISSORS
- FOAM PAINTBRUSH
- **DECOUPAGE** GLUE (E.G, MOD PODGE), MATTE FINISH
- 1 PIECE SCRAPBOOKING CARDSTOCK, SILVER/DARK GRAY
- RULER OR TAPE MEASURE
- CHIPBOARD LETTERS (ENOUGH TO SPELL "GO BOLDLY")
- SPRAY PAINT, METALLIC SILVER
- HOT GLUE GUN

INSTRUCTIONS

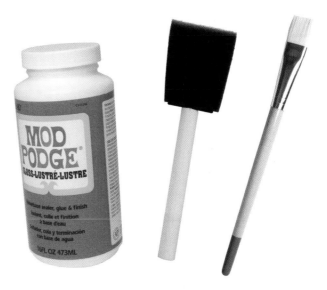

1. Paint the canvas with acrylic paint. Consider combining several shades of paint to get a nice, rich color base. Let the canvas dry for several hours or overnight.

2. Using the pattern from the appendix, trace the delta insignia on the back of your patterned scrapbooking paper and cut it out. When tracing on the back of the paper, make sure to flip the pattern so the insignia will face the right way on the front.

Trekker TIP! FOR A SMOOTHER CUT, MOVE THE PAPER AS YOU CUT, RATHER THAN THE SCISSORS.

3. Load up a paintbrush with Mod Podge and apply the glue to the canvas where you want to place the insignia. While the Mod Podge is still wet, lightly place the insignia on the canvas, adjusting until it's right where you want it. Press the insignia into place and smooth out any air pockets.

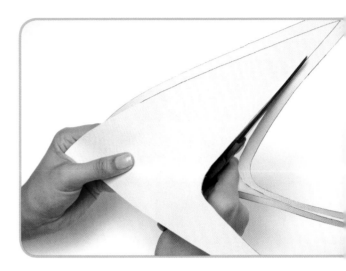

4. Trace the delta insignia on the back of the scrapbooking cardstock. Measure ½ inch in from the outline and draw a second outline. (You can use the original pattern as a guide; just make sure the interior outline is smaller than the first.)

5. Cut along the outside line, and then cut along the inner line to remove the middle of the insignia to create an outline.

6. Apply Mod Podge to the edges of the insignia on the canvas; this is where you'll place the cardstock outline shape. While the Mod Podge is still wet, lightly place the cardstock cutout shape along the edges,

adjusting to properly outline the insignia. Carefully press the outline into place and smooth out any air pockets.

7. Apply a coat of Mod Podge to the entire canvas to seal, and let dry several hours or overnight.

8. Using an even back-and-forth motion, spray-paint the chipboard letters with silver metallic paint, and then let dry several hours or overnight.

9. Adhere the painted chipboard letters to the canvas with a hot glue gun.

The Vulcan saying "Infinite Diversity in Infinite Combinations," or IDIC, celebrates the array of variables in the universe. The corresponding symbol, formed by a silver triangle positioned over a gold circle with a white jewel at the tip of the triangle, is called a *Kol-Ut-Shan*, as mentioned in the *VOY* episode "Gravity." In the *TOS* episode "Is There in Truth No Beauty?" Captain Kirk refers to the icon as "the most revered of all Vulcan symbols." Dr. Miranda Jones goes on to explain the philosophy: "The glory of creation is in its infinite diversity," to which Spock adds, "the way our differences combine to create meaning and beauty."

This simple envelope-style pillowcase features the IDIC symbol to remind you of the infinite opportunities for meaning and beauty in the world around you. Stay true to the original *Kol-Ut-Shan* colors or change it up to make your own accent pillow.

"INFINITE DIVERSITY IN INFINITE COMBINATIONS" ENVELOPE-STYLE PILLOWCASE BY ANGIE PEDERSEN

TOOLS & SUPPLIES

- RULER OR TAPE MEASURE
- SCISSORS
- ½ YARD DARK BLUE FLEECE FABRIC
- ⅓ YARD YELLOW FLEECE FABRIC
- ¼ YARD DARK GRAY FLEECE FABRIC
- ½ YARD **FUSIBLE WEB** (E.G., HEAT'N BOND LITE)–OPTIONAL; ALTERNATIVELY YOU CAN SEW THE APPLIQUÉS ON
- IRON
- SEWING MACHINE
- THREAD TO MATCH FLEECES
- PINS
- LARGE GOLD BUTTON
- PILLOW FORM (THE ONE IN THE EXAMPLE IS 12 INCHES × 16 INCHES)

INSTRUCTIONS

NOTE: The following instructions are based on using a 12-inch × 16-inch pillow form, but you can create a pillowcase for a different-size pillow by adapting the measurements in the patterns and instructions accordingly.

1. Measure and cut the dark blue fleece for the pillow cover. For a 12-inch × 16-inch pillow, the front piece should be 13 inches × 17 inches and the back piece should be 13 inches × 20 inches. (If you're adapting the project for another-size pillow, measure your pillow, then add 1 inch to each side for the front piece and 1 inch to the height and 4 inches to the length for the back piece.)

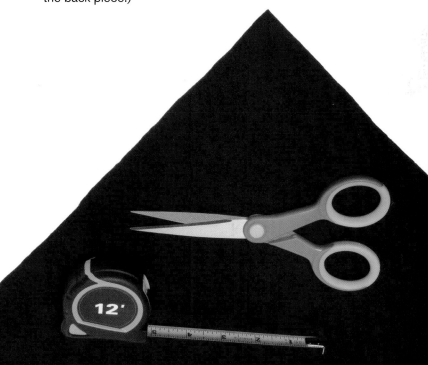

2. Enlarge the IDIC emblem pattern from the appendix by 70 percent (or larger if your pillow is bigger; reduce the pattern if your pillow is smaller) using a photocopier or design editing software and a printer. Following the pattern, cut the smaller circle out of the yellow fleece and then the larger circle around that.

3. Using the pattern from the appendix, cut the triangle piece out of the gray fleece, each side the same length across.

4. Using the fusible web or your sewing machine, attach the circle and triangle pieces to the **right side**

(outward facing side) of the front piece of the pillowcase. If you use fusible web, follow the packaging directions. If all edges don't adhere completely, you can touch them up with an iron or go over the edges with the sewing machine.

5. Cut the back piece of the blue fleece in half widthwise so you have two 13-inch × 10-inch pieces. With right sides together, align the two back pieces with the side edges of the blue front piece, so the back pieces overlap in the middle to create the "envelope flap" opening. Pin around the edges, leaving the envelope flap open in the middle.

6. Sew around all the edges, capturing the envelope flap edges along the way. In the middle of the long side, you will be sewing through three layers of fleece.

7. Turn the pillowcase right side out, making sure to poke out the corners.

8. Hand-sew the button at the top of the triangle.

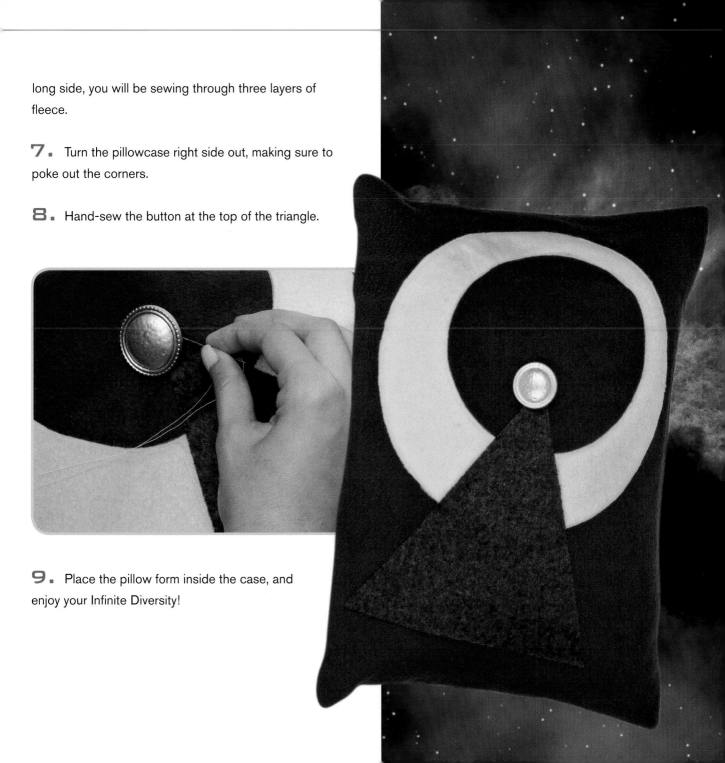

9. Place the pillow form inside the case, and enjoy your Infinite Diversity!

The most recognizable captain in the *Star Trek* franchise, James Tiberius Kirk was born in Iowa. (Although, in the alternate reality established in the 2009 movie *Star Trek*, Kirk was born aboard a medical shuttle fleeing the destruction of the *U.S.S. Kelvin*.) Inspired by his father, he enrolled in Starfleet Academy in his early twenties.

After graduating, Kirk rose swiftly through the ranks. Promoted to captain at the young age of thirty-one, Kirk assumed command of the *Enterprise* after Christopher Pike became fleet captain.

Kirk eventually worked his way up to admiral in *Star Trek: The Motion Picture*. After disobeying the orders of a superior officer in *Star Trek III: The Search for Spock*, he was demoted to captain in *Star Trek IV: The Voyage Home*.

Pay homage to this legendary captain in fuse bead form with this fun, easy project. Make sure to capture Kirk's awesome side (which he might say is all of them).

CAPTAIN JAMES T. KIRK STYLIZED
FUSE BEAD FORM   BY DUSTY TRINKETS

ENSIGN: △△△

TOOLS & SUPPLIES

- SQUARE OR RECTANGULAR PEGBOARD(S)
- FUSE BEADS
- WAX PAPER
- IRON

INSTRUCTIONS

1. Set up your pegboards and your beads. You need:

- 1,283 RED BEADS
- 644 BLACK BEADS
- 798 YELLOW BEADS
- 270 TAN BEADS
- 28 GRAY OR WHITE BEADS
- 358 DARK YELLOW BEADS

2. Each dot in the pattern in the appendix corresponds to a bead. Follow the pattern for placing the beads.

NOTE: Pegboards come in various sizes. You can use one large or multiple small pegboards for this project. If you're using smaller pegboards, you can work through the pattern section by section and iron your pieces together at the end.

3. When you've finished placing the beads, lay wax paper over the fuse beads and iron according to the fuse bead package instructions. Check that all beads have melted before moving your beads off your pegboard. If you're working in pieces, once each piece has cooled, place wax paper over each piece and iron all your sections together.

4. On the back side of your portrait, lay wax paper over the entire piece and iron.

Trekker TIP! LAY THE PORTRAIT UNDER A LARGE BOOK TO FLATTEN OUT ANY CURVED EDGES.

5. Frame and hang your portrait.

PERSONAL LOG

I remember when *TNG* premiered when I was in junior high. Our regular TV was broken (remember those tiny TVs with a dial and no remote? I don't either. I was just asking), and we had to watch the first episode in black and white. My dad recorded the episode on our VHS player, though, so when we got our TV fixed, we got to watch it in glorious 15" low-def color. Q is still one of my favorite villains . . . ranking right behind Khan, of course!

—HEATHER MANN

Produced from 1973 to 1974, *TAS* was the shortest of all the series, with just twenty-two episodes in total. Set during the final year of the *Enterprise*'s five-year mission, the series won a Daytime Emmy for Outstanding Entertainment in a Children's Series in 1975. Veteran writers of *TOS*, as well as well-known science fiction writers, such as David Gerrold, D. C. Fontana, and Larry Niven, penned many of the episodes. Several guest actors from *TOS* reprised their characters as voice roles in *TAS*: Stanley Adams as Cyrano Jones in "More Tribbles, More Troubles"; Roger C. Carmel as Harry Mudd in "Mudd's Passion"; and Mark Lenard as Sarek in "Yesteryear."

Whether you are quenching your thirst with Romulan ale or prune juice ("a warrior's drink," according to Worf), you can be sure these coasters will be a conversation starter— and protect your furniture!

STAR TREK: THE ANIMATED SERIES COASTERS BY ANGIE PEDERSEN

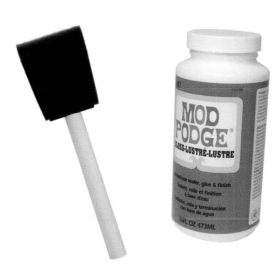

TOOLS & SUPPLIES

- SCISSORS
- CARDSTOCK
- FOAM PAINTBRUSH
- DECOUPAGE GLUE (E.G., MOD PODGE)
- 4 SQUARE PIECES OF CERAMIC TILE (EXAMPLES ARE 4 INCHES × 4 INCHES)
- ADHESIVE-BACKED CORK CUT TO FIT TILE
- ACRYLIC SEALANT (OPTIONAL)

1. Copy or scan and print color copies of the *TAS* images in the appendix. Print them directly onto cardstock or adhere them to cardstock with Mod Podge and trim to size, leaving a narrow white border around the images.

2. Using the foam paintbrush, brush Mod Podge on the back of one of the cardstock pieces, making sure to get the corners and edges.

3. Align the cardstock on and adhere it to a piece of tile, smoothing out any wrinkles or bubbles. Make sure that all the edges and corners firmly adhere.

4. Once you've smoothed out the cardstock, brush a light coat of Mod Podge on top of the image to seal. Allow the Mod Podge to dry 15–30 minutes.

Trekker TIP!

TO VIEW FULL-LENGTH EPISODES OF *TAS*, VISIT HTTP://WWW .STARTREK.COM/VIDEOS/STAR -TREK-THE-ANIMATED-SERIES.

5. Apply two to three more coats of Mod Podge on top of the image, allowing 15–30 minutes of drying time between coats. This will provide a smooth finish and seal on your coasters.

6. Cut adhesive cork to size and adhere to the back of each coaster.

7. Spray a final finish of acrylic sealant on top of the images, to protect them from drink condensation and spills.

8. Repeat steps 1–7 for the rest of the coasters.

As the flagship of the Federation fleet, the *Enterprise* has undergone significant reconstruction through the years. One constant, however, is that it always bears some variation of NCC-1701, except for the ship in *ENT*. (The *Enterprise* NX-01 served as the vessel for the crew of *ENT*.) A sub-letter, such as *A* in NCC-1701-A, helps designate the different registries of the ship.

Among the various series and movies, the *Enterprise* has also been destroyed in a variety of ways. For example, the original *Enterprise*, NCC-1701, was destroyed in *Star Trek III: The Search for Spock*. In *Star Trek Generations*, a Klingon ship commanded by the Duras sisters destroyed the NCC-1701-D, though the saucer section was able to separate in time to save the crew, eventually crash-landing on Veridian III.

This project features the original design of the NCC-1701, though you could use any variation. You could also use the space station in *DS9* or the *U.S.S. Defiant*.

U.S.S. ENTERPRISE GLASS BLOCK
DECORATION BY ANGIE PEDERSEN

CAPTAIN: ▲▲▲

TOOLS & SUPPLIES

- GLASS BLOCK IN A RECTANGLE SHAPE
- PAINTBRUSH
- BLACK GLOSS ENAMEL CRAFT PAINT (SUITABLE FOR PAINTING GLASS)
- THICK BLANK TEMPLATE PLASTIC, FOUND IN THE QUILTING SECTION OF A CRAFT STORE
- EXTRA-FINE-POINT PERMANENT MARKER
- HEATED STENCIL-CUTTING TOOL, X-ACTO KNIFE, OR SHARP, POINTED SCISSORS
- STENCIL ADHESIVE
- MASKING TAPE
- NEWSPRINT (OPTIONAL)
- SPRAY PAINT, METALLIC SILVER
- MINIILGHTS, 20-LIGHT STRING IN WHITE

INSTRUCTIONS

1. Paint the front panel of the glass block black and allow it to dry. The cube may need two coats depending on the paint you use and how opaque you want the panel to be.

2. Using the pattern from the appendix, trace the *Enterprise* shape onto the template plastic with a thin permanent marker.

3. Carefully cut out the ship shape with a heated stencil cutting tool, X-acto knife, or sharp scissors. Be very careful to cut just the shape outline so your stencil will be perfect. Trim your stencil to the size of the front panel of the glass block, approximately 3 inches × 7 inches.

NOTE: If using a heated cutting tool, place the template material on glass to cut. You can use the glass from a photo frame.

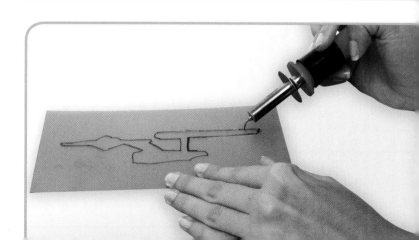

4. Brush stencil adhesive onto the back of the stencil, according to package instructions. Let dry until slightly tacky.

5. Tape your stencil to the front panel of the glass block with masking tape. Make sure not to accidentally peel off any of the black paint with the masking tape. Press down around all edges of the stencil to adhere the stencil adhesive. Mask off the rest of the glass block with newsprint or masking tape.

6. Spray the stencil shape with metallic paint. Allow the paint to dry completely before removing the stencil.

7. Place lights inside glass block and plug them in for full starry effect!

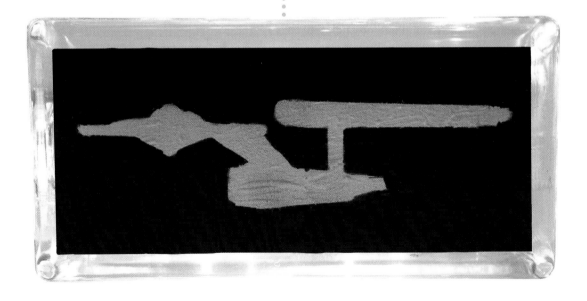

PERSONAL LOG

When I was pregnant with our son, my husband wanted to name him James Tiberius after his favorite *Star Trek* captain. I suggested Thomas as a middle name instead, thinking I would protect my son from relentless teasing in school. (Plus, it was a head nod to William Riker's middle name, as well, so the *Trek* reference was still there.) Even though we did name him James Thomas, my argument was apparently wasted, because my son became such a *Trek* fan that he told me in grade school that he wished I had allowed "Tiberius"!

—ANGIE PEDERSEN

1: TRIBBLES

2: SPOCK MONKEY

4: CAPTAIN KIRK
UNIFORM-INSPIRED
GADGET CASE

5: *STAR TREK: THE NEXT
GENERATION* AMIGURUMI:
PICARD & DATA

3: *STAR TREK* REVERSIBLE
DOG VEST

Not everything about *Star Trek* was hard-core science and facts. Even Spock could appreciate the soothing sounds of a cooing tribble. Explore the softer side of *Star Trek* with these plush and fuzzy projects.

Trekkers and non-Trekkers alike know the iconic *TOS* episode "The Trouble with Tribbles." Merchant Cyrano Jones brings the unassuming furry creatures on board Federation Deep Space Station K-7 to entice trade. The trouble begins when the tribbles start multiplying ("They are born pregnant," declares Dr. Leonard McCoy) and eating a diplomatically important shipment of quadrotriticale, a hybrid grain. Soon Captain Kirk is hip-deep in tribbles—and in a Klingon plot to sabotage the grain shipment.

Tribbles reappear in *TAS* in "More Tribbles, More Troubles," when Jones claims the tribbles he now carries are genetically engineered to be infertile, and in *DS9* in "Trials and Tribble-ations," when Commander Benjamin Sisko and Jadzia Dax travel back in time to stop an assassination attempt on Captain Kirk on Deep Space Station K-7.

Create your own tribble with this quick little project—and have total control over how many replicate in your craft room.

TRIBBLES BY ANGIE PEDERSEN

 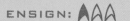

TOOLS & SUPPLIES

- PERMANENT MARKER
- PRINTER PAPER
- SCISSORS
- ½ YARD FAUX FUR FABRIC IN DARK BROWN, LIGHT BROWN, OR WHITE FOR TRADITIONAL TRIBBLES (THIS IS PLENTY TO MAKE MULTIPLE TRIBBLES, BECAUSE THEY DO MULTIPLY!)
- THREAD TO MATCH
- SEWING MACHINE
- FIBERFILL

INSTRUCTIONS

1. Trace or copy the tribble pattern from the appendix onto printer paper and cut it out.

2. Trace the shape onto the back of the faux fur fabric, then flip the pattern over and trace a mirror image right next to what you just traced. You should have two egg shapes with the bases touching when you're finished tracing.

5. Turn tribble right side out and stuff with fiberfill.

3. Carefully cut out the double-oval shape. Make small snips only to the fabric backing so you can keep the long fur hairs intact for a more realistic tribble.

4. With furry sides together, sew around the edges of the tribble. Tuck the fur inside the seam as you sew so as not to catch fur in the stitching. Leave a small opening for turning.

6. Hand-sew the opening shut.

PERSONAL LOG

I got the chance to see *Star Trek: The Exhibition* while visiting the Kennedy Space Center in Florida. The exhibition had props and costumes from all of the *Star Trek* series, but my favorite thing was that I got to sit in the captain's chair from the original *Enterprise*. Who wouldn't want to sit in the captain's chair and pretend to be Captain James T. Kirk?

—KATIE SMITH

As a child, Spock didn't play with toys like this sock monkey; to spend free time not engaged in study would be illogical. However, in the *TOS* episode "Journey to Babel," Spock mentions he did have a pet *sehlat*—a Vulcan bearlike animal with claws and fangs. We meet the *sehlat*, named I-Chaya, in the *TAS* episode "Yesteryear," in which young Spock decides to undergo the *Kahs-wan* ordeal, a ritual by which young Vulcan males prove their manhood by facing the dangers of the desert wilderness alone. I-Chaya saves Spock from a *Le-Matya* attack and is severely wounded. Spock decides to euthanize the animal, instead of letting him suffer. If he had a cute sock monkey like this one, Spock's human half might have been comforted after the loss of his pet *sehlat*.

Spock wore science blue for his uniform, but you can choose any color you like for your little buddy. Enjoy this fun variation on a timeless classic craft!

SPOCK MONKEY BY FINA CARDWELL

ADMIRAL: ▲▲▲

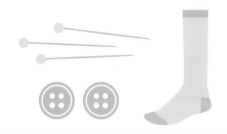

TOOLS & SUPPLIES

- PAIR OF CALF-LENGTH COLORED-HEEL SOCKS
- RULER OR TAPE MEASURE
- WHITE MARKING PENCIL OR PERMANENT MARKER
- THREAD TO MATCH SOCKS
- SEWING MACHINE
- SCISSORS
- FIBERFILL
- CROCHET THREAD TO MATCH SOCKS
- 9-INCH × 12-INCH PIECE OF BLACK FELT
- BLACK THREAD
- BLACK BUTTONS FOR THE EYES
- 9-INCH × 12-INCH PIECE OF LIGHT BLUE FELT, OR ANY OTHER COLOR YOU PREFER FOR THE UNIFORM
- PINS
- SHEET OF IRON-ON TRANSFER PAPER FOR DARK MATERIALS
- IRON

INSTRUCTIONS

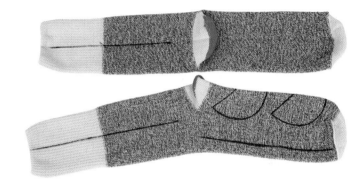

Before you begin creating your Spock monkey, turn both socks inside out and review the pictured markings. Use the template in the appendix for the ears.

TO MAKE THE BODY

1. Using a white marking pencil or permanent marker, mark a line down the center of one sock, starting 3 inches from the colored heel and across to the end of the top. Sew a ½-inch

NOTE: The traditional sock monkey was made from Original Rockford Red Heel® socks, and each pair comes with excellent instructions on how to create one. You can use Red Heel brand socks for your project, or any sock with a colored heel.

double seam on both sides of the line, curving at the edge of the cuff to form the end of the feet.

2. Cut the sock between seams and to within 1½ inches of the colored heel. This leaves an opening in the crotch of the monkey for stuffing.

3. Sew along the raw edges of the crotch with an overcast or zigzag stitch while keeping the hole open. This will keep the edges from fraying while stuffing.

4. Turn the body sock right side out and stuff the head, body, and legs through the crotch opening.

5. Hand-sew the crotch opening closed.

Trekker TIP!

FOR THIS PROJECT, USE A HEAVYWEIGHT THREAD OR CROCHET THREAD FOR STURDIER WORK IN YOUR HAND-SEWING.

TO MAKE THE ARMS/TAIL

1. Using a white marking pencil or permanent marker, mark a line down the center of the second sock. Sew a ½-inch double seam on both sides of the line, curving at the edge of the cuff to form the end of the arms.

2. Cut the sock between the seams to separate the arms and tail. Cut the upper part of the sock into two pieces to form the arms.

3. Turn the arms and tail right side out and stuff.

ASSEMBLY

Assemble the rest of the sock monkey with hand-sewing.

1. To determine where you would like the arms to be on the body, place your hands around the sock body and squeeze lightly to form a neck. This will give you a good idea of how big the head will be and will also leave you a slight indentation that you can use for arm placement. Using heavyweight/crochet thread, sew the arms onto the body.

2. To create a neck, take a long piece of crochet thread and wrap it around the neck area (using the tops of the arms as a guide) and pull to tighten the thread as you wrap. This will form the head and shoulders of the sock monkey.

3. Next, sew the tail on by centering it on the colored heel portion of the bottom. Tuck the raw edges of the tail in and **whipstitch** the tail onto the main sock body.

TO MAKE THE MOUTH

1. Cut the colored heel from the other sock, leaving a slight edge around the colored portion.

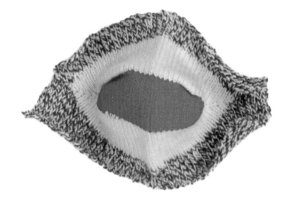

2. Lay the mouth across the bottom portion of the head, aligning the bottom of the mouth piece with the curve of the neck area.

3. Pull and stretch the mouth ends so that the piece lies across the bottom portion of the head. Using crochet thread, whipstitch the mouth to the body starting at one corner of the mouth. Work down around the neck area over to the other corner of the mouth, tucking the raw edges in as you sew so that the beige area of the mouth piece meets the body. Stop here and stuff the mouth. Continue sewing and turning in the raw edges until you get to the original corner where you started sewing.

TO MAKE THE EARS

1. Using the Spock monkey ears pattern in the appendix, cut out two ears from the remaining brown part of the sole of the second sock, maintaining a small seam allowance. Flatten the ears and sew along the outer edges of each ear with a narrow seam allowance. Cut a small slit along the straight edge of the ears, and use this to turn the ears right side out; this will flatten them out. Close up the opening from where you turned them.

2. Sew on the ears, with the pointed portion of the ears at the top. Use the mouth placement as a guide for the ears; the bottoms of the ears will rest at the corners of the mouth piece. This should place them in the middle of the sock if you turn it sideways. Secure them to the head with whipstitches along the front and the back of the ears.

TO MAKE THE HAIR

1. Using the back of your sock monkey's head, measure out a long rectangular piece of black felt, about the width of his head from ear to ear. To estimate the length of the hair piece, hold the felt at the base of his neck where you want the hair to end (long enough to reach the bottoms of his ears) and fold the felt over to the front of his face. Note where the felt crosses at

the crown of his head and fold the felt in half at that point. Cut the felt.

2. Using the hair template in the appendix, place the top of the curve against the top fold of the hair. Using a white marking pencil, trace the curve against the felt and cut. Sew along the curve only. *Do not* sew

down the edges of the hair yet: Leave the sides open so that when you place the hair over Spock's head, the front and back pieces split over his ears.

3. Next, cut a window in the front piece of the hair to allow Spock's face to show: Cut a thin strip next to the ears for his sideburns that are equal length and then cut across the top to meet where the sideburns were cut to create the bangs.

4. Using black thread, sew down all the edges of his hair.

TO MAKE THE EYES/EYEBROWS

1. Using the scrap piece of felt, cut two little strips for his eyebrows and sew those on.

2. Sew on button eyes.

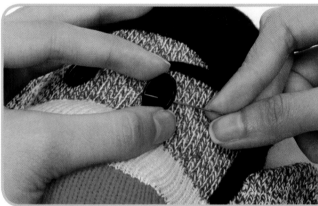

Trekker TIP! IF MAKING THIS FOR CHILDREN UNDER THREE, EMBROIDER THE EYES WITH BLACK THREAD.

TO MAKE THE SHIRT

1. Using the shirt template in the appendix, cut shirt pieces from the light blue felt. Cut the front V-neck shirt piece and the back scoop-neck shirt piece.

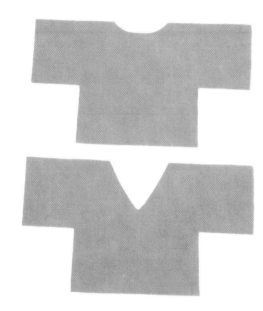

NOTE: Cut out the patterns in paper first and hold these up to your sock monkey for measurement. If you have "overstuffed" your sock monkey, you can adjust the fit of this shirt by widening the side seams on the shirt and lowering the bottom edge of the sleeves.

3. Cut a shorter strip of black felt that is the same width and attach it to the scoop-neck portion of the shirt back. Sew the strip in place.

4. Cut shorter strips of black felt to line the cuffs of the shirtsleeves. Sew the strips in place.

2. Cut one long strip of black felt for the collar of the shirt. Lay the blue shirt pieces right side up in front of you. Fold the strip in half and sew a diagonal seam along the folded edge. Trim away the excess. When the strip is opened, it should form a V. Lay the open strip against the V of the shirt front, pin in place, and sew the black felt to the shirt front.

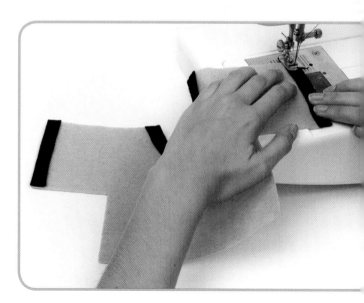

5. After you sew on all the black felt strips, place the shirt pieces with right sides together and sew along the seams indicated on the template. Turn the shirt right side out.

6. Copy or print the *Star Trek* insignia pattern found in the appendix onto iron-on transfer paper. Following the instructions on the iron-on transfer paper packaging, iron the insignia onto the felt shirt.

Trekker TIP! THE IRON-ON PAPERS MADE ESPECIALLY FOR DARK MATERIALS PROVIDE THE BEST COVERAGE.

7. Dress Spock in his new shirt and you're done!

PERSONAL LOG

I'm terrible at favorites. I believe that one can't be fickle about favorites, so I'm hesitant to commit to a single episode or movie (or ice cream flavor for that matter). One thing that *Star Trek* has been for me over the years, despite the geeky reputation of science fiction fans, is a normal social thing. Even before the days of on-demand TV and DVRs, I rarely would set aside a specific time to watch a broadcast TV show, but for *Star Trek* I did. Especially the *DS9* and *VOY* eras. It was social, because it was a household ritual in which we would include friends and visiting family sometimes. Then there were "Trekian" inside jokes and conversational asides with those friends and family. It was more than just the hour the show was on and not nearly the extreme fan caricatures we see portrayed; it was kind of perfect. The ritual continues with my small collection of *Star Trek* Christmas ornaments from Hallmark. I sure don't have them all, but I have plenty, and they are permanently strung on a faux fir lighted garland that I hang every year, even when I can't have a tree because of pets or travel.

—TARA FIELDS

Though rife with different life-forms, most of the *Star Trek* universe avoids mention of pets. One major exception is *ENT*, in which Captain Jonathan Archer (played by Scott Bakula) keeps his pet beagle, Porthos, on board. We learn about his relationship with his pet during the episode "A Night in Sickbay," when Porthos contracts an alien pathogen and Dr. Phlox and Archer spend the night nursing him back to health. Archer explains that Porthos was last in a litter of four male puppies, "the Four Musketeers."

Played by three different performing animals, Porthos often enjoyed in-between-shot tummy rubs and cheese treats from Bakula.

Just as Porthos became part of the *Enterprise* crew, promote your pooch to Starfleet ranks with this adorable reversible dog vest. Work up this project in a deep-space blue and command yellow on the other side, or choose your own color palette.

STAR TREK REVERSIBLE DOG VEST
BY TARA FIELDS

ADMIRAL: ▲▲▲

TOOLS & SUPPLIES

- RULER OR TAPE MEASURE
- PENCIL
- LARGE PIECE OF BUTCHER PAPER (OR TAPE TOGETHER SEVERAL SHEETS OF PRINTER PAPER), BIG ENOUGH TO FIT AROUND YOUR DOG
- SCISSORS
- FLEECE FABRIC IN TWO *STAR TREK* UNIFORM COLORS (E.G., YELLOW AND BLUE) FOR TWO-SIDED VEST, ENOUGH TO WRAP AROUND YOUR DOG
- STRAIGHT PINS
- TAILOR'S MARKING CHALK (OPTIONAL)
- ¼ YARD FLEECE FABRIC, BLACK
- PRINTER PAPER
- SATIN FABRIC, SILVER
- FUSIBLE WEB (E.G., HEAT'N BOND)
- POLY-COTTON BLEND FABRIC, BLACK (TWO SMALL SQUARES, ABOUT 3 INCHES × 3 INCHES EACH)
- THREAD TO MATCH FABRIC
- SEW-ON HOOK AND LOOP TAPE, SUCH AS VELCRO

INSTRUCTIONS

The example pattern from the appendix is designed to be placed on the fold line of your material, so the resulting piece will open up to wrap around your dog.

TO MAKE THE VEST PATTERN

SHAPE

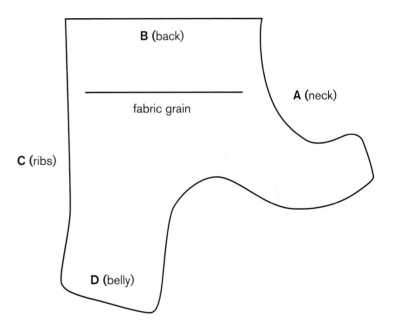

Refer to the guide shape above to help you create your vest pattern. Measure and draw the following on your large piece of butcher paper.

1. **Line A:** Measure your dog's neck loosely (as though measuring for a collar); divide that number in half and add 2 inches. For example, if your dog's neck is 16 inches around, divide 16 by 2 (8 inches) and add 2 inches = 10 inches.

2. **Line B:** Measure from where your dog's collar meets your dog's spine to where you want the vest to end.

3. **Line C:** Measure around your dog's ribs at the bottom point of the vest (the end of line B); divide that number in half and add 2 inches.

4. Draw in the rest of the pattern based on your dog's size—narrower for small-chested dogs, wider for large-chested dogs. The example, based on a pattern for a 50-pound hound dog, uses about 3½ inches for the chest closure (line D) and about 6 inches for the rib area (line C). Notice line D slants to accommodate the slant of the ribs toward the waist; adjust that slant depending on your dog's shape.

5. Cut out paper pattern and wrap around your dog, matching line B to its spine, to verify the fit.

TO CUT THE MATERIAL FOR THE VEST

1. Fold one piece of colored fleece material in half, parallel to the selvage edges.

2. Lay your vest pattern with line B on the fold and pin or mark the outline on the fleece. Cut out the pattern, making sure to snip through both layers.

3. Mark the center of the neckline with a small notch or with a chalk mark.

4. Repeat marking and cutting for the other color of fleece material.

5. Trace the collar pattern from the appendix onto printer paper. Fold the black fleece in half, parallel to the selvage edges, and place the long, straight edge of the pattern on the fold. Pin or mark it with chalk. Cut and mark the center of the long curved sides.

TO MAKE THE INSIGNIA

Create two insignias if you want an insignia on both sides of your vest.

1. Trace the delta insignia from the appendix onto printer paper, about 1¾–2 inches high.

2. Pin the paper pattern to the silver satin fabric and roughly cut out the shape.

3. Trace delta insignia in reverse on the appropriate side of fusible web, per manufacturer's instructions.

4. Trim the fusible web to size, leaving at least ½ inch around all sides.

5. Remove the paper backing and fuse, per manufacturer's instructions, to the back of the silver satin.

6. Trim to your traced insignia pattern line.

7. Following manufacturer's directions, fuse the satin insignia to the black poly-cotton fabric. After fusing, trim the black material, leaving a thin border of black around the outside edge of the satin piece.

8. For extra durability, sew the satin insignia to the black insignia using a short, small zigzag stitch around the satin edge with a thread that blends with the satin.

9. Following manufacturer's instructions, fuse another piece of fusible web on the back of the black fabric. Trim to size.

10. Repeat steps to create another insignia if you want one on each side of your reversible vest.

TO ASSEMBLE THE VEST

1. On the right side of the fleece, select the spot for the insignia. Be sure it's centered from top to bottom so it doesn't get sewn into the seam when you're attaching the vest pieces. This is a good time to try the vest on your dog to verify placement of the insignia when the vest is worn.

2. Fuse an insignia to the right side of each color of fleece and then reinforce with a short, small zigzag stitch around the black part of the insignia.

3. Fold the collar piece in half lengthwise with right sides out. Line up the center of the collar with the center of the vest (line B). Pin baste the collar to one vest piece, right sides together, and sew using a ¼-inch seam.

4. Pin vest pieces right sides together (collar on the inside) and sew a ½-inch seam, leaving 7–8 inches open for turning. (Make sure that you don't sew the insignia into the seam!)

5. Trim one layer of the fleece close to the seam, leaving the opening untrimmed. **Notch and clip** curves; trim corners.

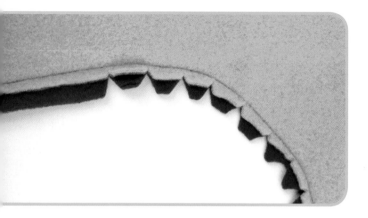

6. Turn the vest right side out, taking care to fully turn the seam.

7. At the opening, fold the fleece under ½ inch and pin, making sure that each color shows only on one side, then topstitch ¼ inch around the entire vest.

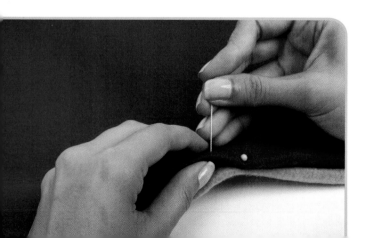

(Again, make sure you don't sew through your insignia.) Use a different color thread on your bobbin to match the fleece on the bottom for a cleaner look.

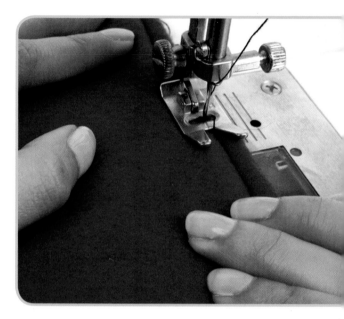

8. Using your vest as a guide, cut the hook and loop fastener for the chest and rib closures; they should fit just within the top stitching of the vest. Round the corners slightly for durability and comfort.

9. Position and pin your hook and loop pieces to your vest. Verify your bobbin thread matches the material on the underside of your vest. You may have to change bobbin colors to accomplish this.

1 0. Trim all your threads and dress your dog to boldly go where no one has gone before!

Trekker TIP!

THIS IS A WARM JACKET; KEEP AN EYE ON YOUR DOG SO SHE OR HE DOESN'T OVERHEAT.

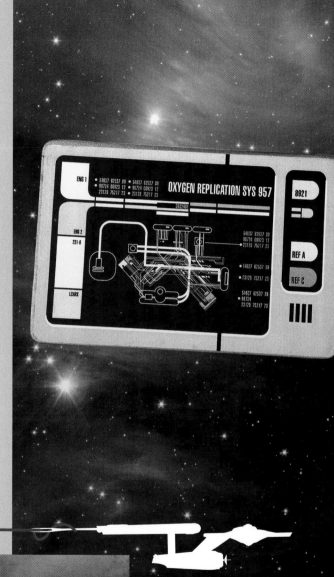

Device manufacturers were way behind the innovative minds at *Star Trek*: The PADD (Personal Access Display Device) first appeared on *TOS* in episodes such as "The Man Trap" and "The Menagerie," about forty-five years before tablet computers hit the market. Initially, they were large wedge-shaped devices, operated almost exclusively by use of a stylus and usually toted by yeomen bearing duty rosters and status reports in search of command approvals.

As with many gadgets, the PADD received a significant upgrade in design and function in *TNG*, its sleek touch screen interface no longer requiring a cumbersome stylus for direction. Although primarily used for data entry and retrieval, some PADDs allowed users to draw up ship schematics and even create artwork.

You can protect your modern-day digi-devices in *Star Trek* style with this gadget case made with sturdy wool felt and emblazoned with a delta shield.

CAPTAIN KIRK UNIFORM—INSPIRED GADGET CASE BY SARAH DUNN

CAPTAIN: ΛΛΛ

TOOLS & SUPPLIES

- SCISSORS
- ¼ YARD DARK YELLOW WOOL FELT (36-INCH WIDTH)
- ¼ YARD LIGHT GRAY WOOL FELT (36-INCH WIDTH) FOR LINING
- BLACK WOOL FELT FOR NECK PIECE (ROUGHLY THE SIZE OF A POSTCARD)
- SILVER OR DARK GRAY WOOL FELT FOR DELTA SHIELD (3 INCHES × 3 INCHES SQUARE)
- SEWING MACHINE
- THREAD
- SCISSORS
- PINS
- IRON
- INVISIBLE/CLEAR THREAD (OPTIONAL)

INSTRUCTIONS

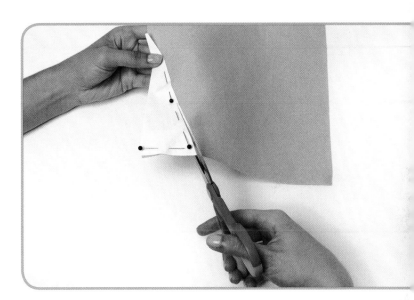

1. Using the pattern in the appendix, cut one front, one back, and two sleeve pieces from dark yellow felt, making sure the sleeve pieces mirror each other. Cut two more pieces of the back pattern from the light gray felt, and trim ⅛ inch from each side; this will be the lining. Cut the neck piece from the black felt and the delta shield from dark gray felt.

Trekker TIP!

WOOL FELT HOLDS UP BETTER THAN CRAFT FELT, SEWS EASIER, DOESN'T FRAY, AND DOESN'T GET FUZZY OVER TIME. WOOL-RAYON BLENDS ARE BEST AND COME IN MANY COLORS!

Trekker TIP!

WHEN PINNING, LAY THE BACK PIECE FLAT AND PLACE THE SLEEVE PIECES IN THE COR-NERS. THEN WHEN YOU LAY THE FRONT PIECE ON TOP AND PIN, THE SLEEVE PIECES WILL BE STRAIGHT.

2. Starting with the sleeves, sew all pieces of the uniform front. The front will overlap the sleeve and neck pieces by ¼ inch, but stitch ⅛ inch from the edge. After sewing the front piece together, use small scissors to clip the corners of the sleeves where they meet the neck. Also sew on the delta shield at this time.

3. With right sides together, at the top only, sew one lining piece to the uniform front and the other lining piece to the uniform back using a ¼-inch seam allowance.

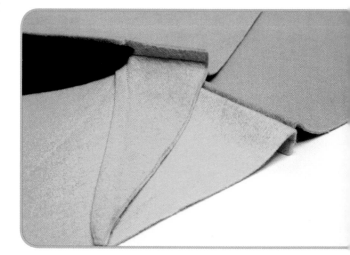

4. Pin the right sides of the front and back (with lining attached) together so you have two long pieces. Starting approximately 1 inch in from one corner of the lining, sew all the way around the edges using a ¼-inch seam allowance until 1 inch after the opposite corner of lining; this will leave about a 6-inch opening in the bottom of the lining. Clip all four corners.

5. Pull the whole case inside out through the opening in the lining. (Be careful not to stretch the felt!) Turn the lining into the case and iron the edges where the uniform and lining meet. Topstitch around the edge. (You can use invisible/clear thread all the way around, or use yellow on the uniform, changing to black thread at the neckline.)

6. Stitch the opening in the bottom of the lining closed. Iron the whole case so it lies flat.

NOTE: To make this case for other tablets, e-readers, and even phones, size the pattern so that it is 1½ inches wider and 1¼ inches taller than your gadget. If your device is thick, such as a laptop, add more width to the pattern equal to the depth of your item in addition to the 1½ inches to accommodate the extra bulk.

The only nonbiological crew member, Lieutenant Commander Data (played by Brent Spiner) is a fully functional android who serves as chief operations officer on *TNG*. Created by Dr. Noonien Soong and lacking the ability to feel emotion, Data constantly seeks to learn more about the human experience, studying literature and music, and even caring for a cat.

We learn more about Data's family in the episode "Brothers," when Spiner plays three roles: Data, Dr. Soong, and Data's antisocial android brother, Lore.

The potential face for sentient robots in the future, Data was inducted into Carnegie Mellon University's Robot Hall of Fame at the Carnegie Science Center in Pittsburgh, Pennsylvania, in 2008.

Channel your Dr. Soong and create your own Data with this quick crochet pattern. He may not be "fully functional," but this amigurumi figure sure is cute. You can also create a little Picard to have interstellar adventures with.

STAR TREK: THE NEXT GENERATION AMIGURUMI: PICARD AND DATA

BASED ON A PATTERN BY HOPE FURNO

CAPTAIN: ▲▲▲

TOOLS & SUPPLIES

- F CROCHET HOOK
- WORSTED WEIGHT YARN, CREAM
- WORSTED WEIGHT YARN, GOLD METALLIC (OPTIONAL)
- FIBERFILL
- 2 7-MILLIMETER BUTTONS FOR EYES
- 2 GOLD BRADS
- BLACK PERMANENT MARKER
- TAPESTRY NEEDLE
- BULKY WEIGHT YARN, BLACK
- WORSTED WEIGHT YARN, BLACK
- WORSTED WEIGHT YARN, RED OR MAROON
- WORSTED WEIGHT YARN, MUSTARD YELLOW
- SCISSORS
- FELT, SILVER OR GRAY
- FELT, GOLD OR YELLOW
- SEWING NEEDLE
- SEWING THREAD, CREAM

INSTRUCTIONS

TO MAKE THE HEAD

Use cream-colored yarn for Picard and gold metallic for Data (or use a paler shade of cream yarn).

- In a **magic ring**, sc 6 around (6 stitches at end of round)

Round 1: sc 2 in each stitch around (12 stitches at end of round)

Trekker TIP!

ABBREVIATIONS
(SEE THE GLOSSARY FOR A DEFINITION OF EACH STITCH)
SC: **SINGLE CROCHET**
DEC: **SINGLE DECREASE STITCH**
SL ST: **SLIP STITCH**

Round 2: *sc 1 in next sc, sc 2 in next sc; repeat from * 5 more times (18 stitches at end of round)

Round 3: *sc 1 in each of next 2 sc, sc 2 in next sc; repeat from * 5 more times (24 stitches at end of round)

Rounds 4–8: sc around (24 stitches)

Round 9: *sc 1 in each of the next 2 sc, dec; repeat from * 5 more times (18 stitches at end of round)

FOR PICARD

Stuff the head with fiberfill at this point before continuing.

Round 10: *sc 1, dec; repeat from * 5 more times (12 stitches at end of round)

Round 11: dec around (6 stitches at end of round). Fasten off, leaving a long tail to attach head to body Sew button eyes onto head

FOR DATA

Stop at Round 9 to add eyes and hair:

• Use permanent marker to draw pupils in center of gold brads.

• Insert brads into unfilled head and open prongs to attach.

• Using a tapestry needle and black bulky weight yarn, stitch "strands" of hair onto unfilled head.

After hair is attached, stuff with fiberfill and finish decreasing crochet stitches to close head:

Round 10: *sc 1, dec; rep from * 5 more times (12 stitches at end of round)

Round 11: dec around (6 stitches at end of round); fasten off leaving a long tail to attach the head to body.

TO MAKE THE BODY

• Using black yarn, in a magic ring, sc 6 around (6 stitches at end of round)

Round 1: sc 2 in each stitch around (2 stitches at end of round)

Round 2: *sc 1 in next sc, sc 2 in next sc; repeat from * 5 more times (18 stitches at end of round)

Round 3: *sc 1 in each of next 2 sc, sc 2 in next sc; repeat from * 5 more times (24 stitches at end of round)

Rounds 4–5: sc around (24 stitches)

• Switch to red/maroon yarn for Picard or mustard yellow yarn for Data before continuing.

Round 6: *sc 8, dec; repeat from * twice (18 stitches at end of round)

Round 7–8: sc around (18 stitches)

Round 9: sc 3, dec, sc 6, dec, sc 5 (16 stitches at end of round)

• Switch to black yarn for shoulders for both Picard and Data

Round 10: sc 3, dec, sc 5, dec, sc 1, dec (12 stitches at end of round)

Round 11: With black, sc around, sl st and fasten off, and then stuff

TO MAKE THE BADGE

With sharp scissors, cut a small triangle from the silver/gray felt, then cut an even smaller triangle out of the bottom of the triangle you just made. Cut a small circle out of the gold/yellow felt. Hand-stitch the triangle to the middle of the circle.

TO ASSEMBLE

1. Using the head's long yarn tail, attach the head to body.

2. Hand-stitch the felt comm badge to body.

Trekker TIP!

YOU CAN USE THE SAME BASE PATTERN FOR PICARD TO CREATE OTHER MEMBERS OF THE *ENTERPRISE* CREW!

I grew up in a Trekker household. We used to have this rule that you couldn't eat pizza without watching *Star Trek* and you couldn't watch *Star Trek* without eating pizza. So one to three times a week, all eight members of my family would pile into the kitchen to help make my dad's amazing homemade pizza, and then cram onto our two living room couches to watch *Star Trek*. Our family's favorite series was *VOY* (besides *TOS*, of course), and I especially loved the holodeck episodes.

—HOPE FURNO

1: VULCAN HAT

2: COMIC BOOK LOW-TOP SNEAKERS

4: GEORDI LA FORGE VISOR AND SPOCK SAFETY VISOR SLEEP MASKS

5: TRICORDER PURSE

3: STARFLEET UNIFORM APRON

*S*TAR *TREK* STYLE ISN'T ONLY FOR CONVENTIONS. WORK SOME *STAR TREK* COSTUME PLAY INTO YOUR DAILY WARDROBE BY DONNING A VULCAN HAT OR THROWING ON A UNIFORM APRON WHILE WHIPPING UP DINNER!

One of the more memorable Spock episodes is "Spock's Brain" from the third season of *TOS*. In this episode, an alien female beams aboard the *Enterprise* and, after rendering the rest of the crew unconscious, surgically removes Spock's brain. Dr. McCoy informs Captain Kirk that they have twenty-four hours to locate and replace the Vulcan's brain before his body dies.

Following the alien ship's ion trail, the crew finds the mysterious woman on the planet Sigma Draconis VI, and McCoy is able to use the hatlike Great Teacher device, left by the ancient technological beings that once inhabited the planet, to provide him with the knowledge of how to replace Spock's brain.

Unlike the Great Teacher, this Vulcan hat won't help you learn brain surgery. But it is perfect for costume play, as well as for keeping your head and ears toasty warm. No promises whether it will also prohibit aliens from removing your brain.

VULCAN HAT

HAT BY ANGIE PEDERSEN; EARS DESIGNED BY SHOVE MINK

CAPTAIN: ▲▲▲

TOOLS & SUPPLIES

- L CROCHET HOOK
- BULKY WEIGHT YARN (E.G., LION BRAND HOMETOWN YARN), BLACK
- STITCH MARKER (OPTIONAL)
- SCISSORS
- G CROCHET HOOK
- COTTON YARN IN DESIRED COLOR FOR EARS, SPORT WEIGHT
- TAPESTRY NEEDLE

INSTRUCTIONS

All rounds worked in continuous rounds; do not turn or slip stitch to join rounds.

HAT

- Using L hook and black yarn, work 8 hdc in a magic ring.
  Round 1: Work 2 hdc in each stitch (16 total at end of round)
  Round 2: Work 1 hdc in first stitch, then 2 hdc in next stitch; repeat to beginning of round (24 total at end of round)
  Round 3: Work 1 hdc in first two stitches, then 2 hdc in next stitch; repeat to beginning of round (32 at end of round)
  Round 4: Work 1 hdc in first three stitches, then 2 hdc in next stitch; repeat to beginning of round (40 at end of round)
  Round 5: Work 1 hdc in first four stitches, then 2 hdc in next stitch; repeat to beginning of round (48 at end of round)
  Round 6+: Continue working in the round until hat measures 7½ inches from top to bottom.
- Once you reach the desired length for the crown of the hat,

Trekker TIP!

ABBREVIATIONS
(SEE THE GLOSSARY FOR A DEFINITION OF EACH STITCH)
  HDC: **HALF DOUBLE CROCHET**
  SC: **SINGLE CROCHET**
  CH: **CHAIN**
  INC: **INCREASE STITCH** (OR ADD ONE STITCH)
  STS: **STITCHES**
  SK: **SKIP**

work 24 hdc, ch 1, turn. You will work the remaining rows back and forth in a rectangle to form the nape of the neck.

Rows 1–4: 24 hdc, ch 1, turn

Row 5: Decrease 1, 22 hdc, decrease 1

• Cut yarn and bind off; work in loose end.

Magic Ring

Round 2

EARS (MAKE 2)

The pattern is worked continuously in the round until row 11, after which you will work back and forth.

• Using G hook, work sc 6 in a magic ring

Rounds 1–2: sc 6

Round 3: [sc 1, inc] three times (9 sc total at end of the round)

Rounds 4–5: sc 9

Round 6: [sc 2, inc] three times (12 sc total at end of the round)

Round 7–8: sc 12

Round 9: [sc 3, inc] three times (15 sc total at end of the round)

Round 10: sc 15

Row 11: sc 8

Rows 12–14: ch 1, turn, sc 8 across

Row 15: Skip first st, sc in next 7 sts (7 sc at end of row)

Magic Ring

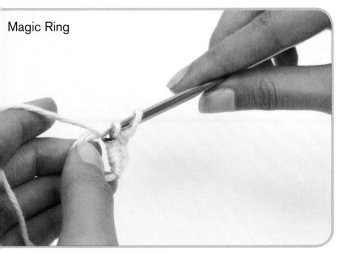

Rounds 1–2

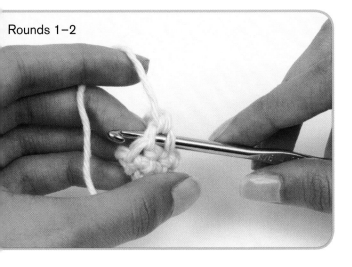

Round 3

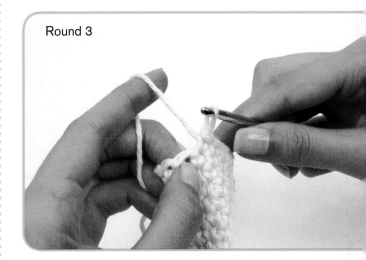

Rows 12–14

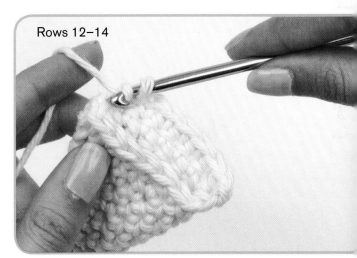

Row 16: Skip first st, sc in next 6 sts (6 sc at end of row)

Row 17: Skip first st, sc in next 5 sts (5 sc at end of row)

Row 19

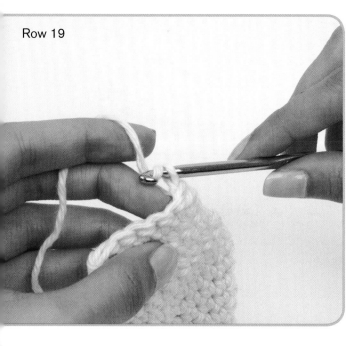

Bind Off

Row 18: Skip first st, sc in next st, sk next st, sc in next 2 sts (3 sc at end of row)

Row 19: Skip fist st, sc in next 2 sts (2 sc at end of row)

Row 20: Skip first st, sc in next st (1 sc at end of row)

• Bind off, leaving a long tail. Fold up the bottom flap formed by the decreases on row 18 and stitch in place with tapestry needle. Place each ear on top of the hat where ears naturally sit, and stitch on with tapestry needle.

PERSONAL LOG

I go to *Star Trek* conventions for the people. It started as an interest in the *Star Trek* shows and movies and their stars, but it evolved into something greater. It became like a family reunion. Loving *Star Trek* is a shared experience. When I started attending conventions I realized most of the activities were very passive in nature. Sit and watch a celebrity talk. Stand in line and get an autograph. I wanted to build active memories. By hosting crafting workshops, I hoped to provide an activity that offered lasting memories—all for free! I do it all for the little girls who high-five me and tell me it was their favorite part of the convention. I do it for the newlyweds on their honeymoon making their first craft together that they will hang in their new home. Everyone deserves to take something home regardless of their income. I take home the best gift of all: knowing that I provided some happiness. I hope years from now, that five-year-old girl will look at her craft and remember her first convention. Just like *Star Trek* does, crafts can inspire curiosity and confidence. My warmest *Star Trek* memories are the ones when I know I've encouraged that.

—MARY CZERWINSKI

Over the years, the *Star Trek* universe has spawned multiple comic book and graphic novel titles, each bringing more depth to the *Star Trek* story lines—for example, with backstories on characters like Chekov and Uhura.

The history of the comic books' distribution is as varied as a crew's away missions. Gold Key was the first to distribute *Star Trek* comic books, from 1967 to 1979, followed by a variety of distributors such as Marvel, DC Comics, Malibu Comics, Tokyopop, and IDW Publishing.

Give your favorite canvas sneakers a funky, cool vibe with the help of some *Star Trek* comic panels. Does the idea of cutting up comic books make you cringe? If so, you can scan images and print them out on fabric, though the look is slightly different: The comic book pages have brighter, crisper colors and text; printed fabric has a more weathered look.

COMIC BOOK LOW-TOP SNEAKERS
BY ANGIE PEDERSEN

TOOLS & SUPPLIES

- PAIR OF CANVAS SNEAKERS (OLD OR NEW)
- *STAR TREK* COMIC BOOKS
- SCISSORS
- DECOUPAGE GLUE (E.G., MOD PODGE), MATTE FINISH
- FOAM PAINTBRUSH

INSTRUCTIONS

1. Choose the comic book images you would like to use on your shoes. Hold the pages up to the shoes so you can get an idea of the space you have to work with. Cut out the images you want to use.

4. Once all the images are in place, brush a generous layer of Mod Podge onto the top of the paper to seal it.

ANOTHER LOOK: INKJET PRINTABLE FABRIC

1. Scan the images you want to use on your shoes into your computer. Using a graphic editing program,

2. Using the paintbrush, apply a generous amount of Mod Podge to the **wrong side** of the paper and press it into place on the shoe. Carefully smooth out any bubbles and creases. Fold and trim the paper along the shoe edges to make a clean line.

3. Repeat steps 1 and 2 for all areas of both shoes you want to cover.

Trekker TIP! TO MAKE YOUR NEW SNEAKERS LAST, AVOID WEARING THEM IN THE RAIN OR GETTING THEM WET.

NOTE: Test the printed images for colorfastness before you apply them to shoes. Apply a thin coat of Mod Podge to a section of printed fabric. If the color runs or becomes blurry, you may not want to use printed fabric on your shoes. If the color stays true, you're good to go.

resize the images to fit the areas on your shoes you want to cover.

2. Using a color inkjet printer, print the images on inkjet printable fabric. Trim the images to size.

3. Follow instructions from step 2 on page 78.

While most of the Starfleet vessels rely upon replicators to feed their crews, the crew of the *U.S.S. Voyager* dines on unique meals lovingly handcrafted by the jovial Talaxian Neelix.

Neelix draws upon his adventures as a scavenger and a merchant in his cooking. He uses fresh produce grown in one of the shuttle bays by his girlfriend, Kes, and his knowledge of nearby planets' flora and fauna to create distinctive dishes for the crew's meals. Despite good-natured ribbing from the crew regarding his questionable cooking skills, he revels in his culinary concoctions and takes pride in his role as chef, creating his own "uniform" of a brightly colored apron and voluminous chef hat.

While this apron might not appeal to Neelix's flamboyant sense of style, it can help you showcase your love of all things *Trek* while in the kitchen or even in the craft room. To adhere to Starfleet protocol, stick with red, blue, or yellow fabric.

STARFLEET UNIFORM APRON
BY KATIE SMITH

ENSIGN: ⋀⋀⋀

TOOLS & SUPPLIES

- RULER OR TAPE MEASURE
- SCISSORS
- 1 YARD OF COTTON FABRIC, BLACK
- IRON
- 1 YARD OF COTTON FABRIC, RED, BLUE, OR YELLOW
- PINS
- SEWING MACHINE
- THREAD TO MATCH
- GOLD TRIM, ABOUT 13 INCHES LONG
- FUSIBLE WEB (E.G., HEAT'N BOND)
- SMALL SCRAP OF GOLD FABRIC (FOR INSIGNIA)
- FABRIC MARKER, BLACK (OPTIONAL)
- BLACK GROSGRAIN RIBBON, ABOUT 2½ YARDS

INSTRUCTIONS

1. Measure and cut out the black fabric piece: 13 inches at the top, 21 inches at the bottom, 18 inches at the sides.

2. From your black fabric also cut a 10-inch-long V shape for the collar, about 2 inches wide. You want a long, shallow V shape. Iron a ¼-inch seam along the top and bottom edges of the V shape.

3. Measure and cut out the colored fabric piece: 10 inches at the top, 13 inches at the bottom, 14 inches at the sides.

4. Pin the V onto the top of your apron and cut out the colored fabric that sticks above the V shape. Fold the ironed edge over the top edge of the apron and pin the V and apron together. Using a **straight stitch**, sew the V down onto the apron on the top and bottom edges of the V.

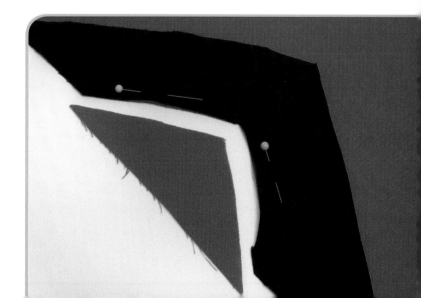

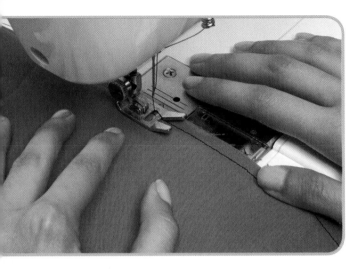

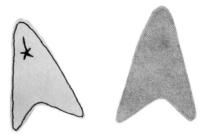

7. Using the pattern in the appendix, trace the insignia onto the paper side of the fusible web. Iron it to a piece of gold fabric according to package directions, and then cut out the insignia.

8. Iron your insignia onto the left breast of your apron with the fusible web adhesive side down.

5. Line up the bottom of your colored piece with the top of your black piece, right sides together, and sew them to form your apron.

6. Sew gold trim across the middle of your apron where the black and colored fabrics meet.

9. Using a **satin stitch**, appliqué the insignia to your apron, going around the edges. You can either appliqué on the black star or draw it on using a fabric marker.

1 0. Iron a ¼-inch seam around all of the edges on your apron, pinning it down as you go.

1 1. Using a straight stitch, sew the finished seam around your apron, going around all four sides. Remove the pins.

1 2. From the black ribbon, cut three straps: one neck strap about 25 inches long, and two side straps, each about 30 inches long—but you may need to adjust the length of these depending on your size.

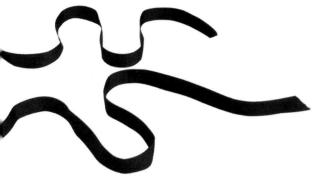

1 3. On the back of your apron, pin the neck strap to the top two corners. Sew down the ends and remove the pins.

1 4. On the back of your apron, pin the side straps to the sides of your apron, just under where the colored fabric meets the black fabric. Sew down ends and remove pins.

One of the most striking things about *TNG* chief engineer Commander Geordi La Forge is his VISOR—Visual Instrument and Sensory Organ Replacement: Without it he is completely blind. Attached at his temples via implants connected directly to his brain, among other things, the VISOR allows La Forge to "see" throughout the electromagnetic spectrum, from heat and infrared through visible light to radio waves.

Spock also sports a visor of sorts, in the *TOS* episode "Is There in Truth No Beauty?" though his is more of the safety-goggle variety. He uses his to protect himself from the sight of the Medusan ambassador's madness-inducing hideous form.

These visors won't help you analyze a Crystalline Entity or prevent insanity, but they could help you get a better night's sleep— or just add some sparkle to your cosplay. Whatever your goal, a few quick steps and you'll soon *see* what fun projects they are.

GEORDI LA FORGE VISOR AND SPOCK SAFETY VISOR SLEEP MASKS BY MARY CZERWINSKI

TOOLS & SUPPLIES

- FABRIC SCISSORS
- RULER OR TAPE MEASURE
- LIGHT-COLORED QUILTED FABRIC
- LIGHT-COLORED THREAD
- NEEDLE
- ⅜-INCH ELASTIC
- SILVER LAMÉ FABRIC
- DRITZ FRAY CHECK (OPTIONAL)
- FABRIC GLUE
- BLACK PERMANENT MARKER
- GLUE

FOR GEORDI LA FORGE VISOR

- GOLD LAMÉ FABRIC

FOR SPOCK SAFETY MASK

- RED LAMÉ FABRIC

INSTRUCTIONS

GEORDI LA FORGE VISOR

1. Using fabric scissors, cut out an 8¼-inch-wide × 1-inch-tall rectangle from the light-colored quilted fabric. The quilted fabric will have batting inside of it.

2. Using the needle and light-colored thread, sew the edges of the quilted fabric together so the batting no longer shows.

3. Cut a 9-inch piece of elastic (make it longer or shorter, if necessary, depending on your head size) and sew it to the back side of the rectangle, equal distance from the top and bottom. Make sure to do multiple stitches so that it will remain secure when stretching and pulling on it.

4. Cut out an 8¼-inch × 1-inch piece of silver lamé.

5. Cut out a 7-inch × ¾-inch piece of gold lamé.

6. Attach the silver rectangle to the front of the quilted fabric using a light coating of fabric glue.

7. Attach the gold lamé rectangle in the middle of the silver rectangle using a light coating of fabric glue.

8. Using a black permanent marker, draw thick lines ½ centimeter (5 millimeters) apart.

9. For a finishing touch, cut out two small circles of gold lamé and glue them to the ends of the visor.

> **NOTE:** Lamé fabric frays easily when being cut or handled. You can purchase a fray prevention product like Dritz Fray Check to help avoid this. Use it sparingly along the edges to avoid staining.

SPOCK SAFETY MASK

1. Using fabric scissors, cut out a 6½-inch × 2½-inch rounded rectangle from the light-colored quilted fabric. The quilted fabric will have batting inside of it.

2. Using the needle and light-colored thread, sew the edges of the quilted fabric together so the batting no longer shows.

3. Cut a 9-inch piece of elastic (make it longer or shorter, if necessary, depending on your head size) and sew it to the back side of the rectangle, equal distance from the top and bottom. Make sure to do multiple stitches so that it will remain secure when stretching and pulling on it.

4. Cut out a 7-inch × 3-inch rectangle from the silver lamé.

5. Cut out a 5½-inch × 2-inch rectangle from the red lamé.

6. Using a light coating of fabric glue, attach the silver rectangle to the front side of the quilted fabric.

7. Attach the red rectangle centered on top of the silver piece using a light coating of fabric glue.

8. Optional: Spray the edges sparingly with Dritz Fray Check.

Designed to scan, analyze, and record data, the tricorder is a handheld device that made its first appearance in the *TOS* episode "The Enemy Within."

The black rectangular gadget analyzes a variety of materials, including geological, meteorological, and biological specimens. There are also specialized variations of the device specifically for engineering and medical needs. Dr. McCoy uses the medical sensor probe to help determine the health of his patients, often leading him to proclaim, "He's dead, Jim."

Make your own tricorder for daily use! Using a combination of two different crafting techniques—freezer paper stenciling and sewing—this is a truly craftacular project.

TRICORDER PURSE

BY ASHLEY LOTECKI

ADMIRAL: ▲▲▲

TOOLS & SUPPLIES

- SCISSORS
- PRINTER PAPER
- VINYL, BLACK
- IRON-ON INTERFACING
- HOLOGRAPHIC BLUE SPANDEX
- SCREEN MESH
- PADDED FOAM
- BLUE FELT
- BUTCHER PAPER OR FREEZER PAPER
- MASKING TAPE
- CUTTING BOARD
- IRON
- IRON-SAFE PAPER (PLAIN OR PARCHMENT)
- SILVER SILK-SCREEN INK (OR PAINT THAT WOULD WORK ON VINYL)
- PAINTBRUSH
- SILVER AND BLACK PERMANENT MARKERS FOR TOUCH-UPS
- PINS
- SEWING MACHINE
- TEFLON PRESSER FOOT (OPTIONAL: THIS WILL KEEP THE SEWING MACHINE PRESSER FOOT FROM STICKING TO THE VINYL)
- BLACK THREAD
- 3 SILVER EYELETS
- 3 SILVER STUDS
- PENCIL
- EYELET PUNCH (OPTIONAL)
- X-ACTO KNIFE OR CRAFT BLADE
- STRONG GLUE (IT MUST BE ABLE TO HOLD STYROFOAM TO VINYL)
- 7-INCH BLACK ZIPPER
- 2 PIECES OF 1-INCH-WIDE BLACK NYLON WEBBING, EACH CUT 3 INCHES LONG
- 2 1-INCH SILVER D RINGS
- STRAP

INSTRUCTIONS

1. Copy or scan and print all of the pattern pieces from the appendix onto printer paper: back tricorder, front tricorder, video screen, speaker, circle, rectangle. Cut the patterns out of the paper and use them for the following:

- Front tricorder: Cut 1 front in black vinyl and 1 in iron-on interfacing.
- Back tricorder: Cut 1 back in black vinyl.
- Video screen: Cut 1 in holographic blue spandex and 1 in iron-on interfacing.
- Circle: Cut 1 in screen mesh.
- Square: Cut 1 in padded foam.
- Rectangle: Cut 1 in blue felt.

2. Iron the video screen interfacing piece to the back of the video screen fabric piece.

3. Copy or scan and print the butcher paper template from the appendix and cut around the outside edge. Place the template pattern in front of the butcher paper (which should be shiny side down) and use masking tape to secure both layers on a flat, hard surface, like a cutting board, that you can cut on. Cut out the gray sections; these will be where you apply the silver paint.

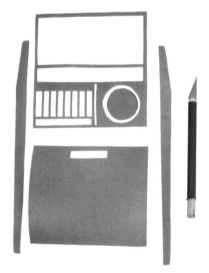

4. Preheat your iron to the synthetic setting, with steam completely off. If you are unsure of your iron's settings, start low and test out what heat setting works

with a scrap piece of vinyl and scrap piece of butcher paper. If the heat is too low, the butcher paper will not stick; too high and the vinyl will melt, which could damage your iron or burn you. Be careful!

and slowly sliding it left to right. Then pick it up to start at the right again, moving lower with each pass. Once the template is fully adhered, turn your iron off and let the template sit until it is cool to touch.

5. Place the front tricorder vinyl piece on your ironing surface and lay the butcher paper template on it (shiny side down). The only areas that should be visible now are the ones that will eventually be painted silver. Put down a piece of blank printer paper or parchment paper over the design to keep the vinyl from sticking to the iron and to stop the butcher paper template from moving around. Apply the iron to the surface, carefully

6. The butcher paper template should now reveal where to apply the silk-screen ink/paint. Paint the open areas. Be careful around the edges of the butcher paper so you don't accidentally separate it from

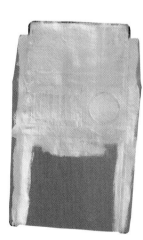

the vinyl with your paintbrush. Depending on your brand of ink or paint, you may have to do multiple layers to achieve solid silver. Use your discretion. Once you finish your final layer of paint, let it dry completely following the manufacturer's instructions.

7. Carefully pull the butcher paper off the vinyl and discard it. To set the ink, iron from the back of the vinyl following the manufacturer's instructions.

8. You should now have crisp silver edges where you painted. If you notice some bleeding, don't worry! You can use your black and silver permanent markers to touch up the edges. (Be sure to test them on a

NOTE: Remember that vinyl will melt at high temperatures so use a paper buffer to protect the vinyl and, if necessary, use a lower heat setting.

scrap piece of vinyl beforehand to make sure the color doesn't bleed.)

9. Pin the video screen piece to the front tricorder piece, using the original paper pattern as a placement guide. Machine sew the piece 1/16 of an inch from the edge, or as close to the edge as you feel comfortable.

10. Next, pin the circle piece to the front tricorder piece, using the original paper pattern as a placement guide. Machine-sew the piece with a ¼-inch seam allowance.

11. Use the front tricorder paper pattern to mark where to place the eyelets and studs. You can use a dull pencil to make a mark into the middle of each circle and then put the pattern aside. To make the holes, you can use an eyelet punch or you can carefully cut

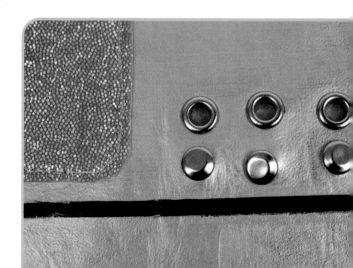

a small X into the fabric with a blade. Apply the three eyelets to the top and three studs to the bottom following manufacturer's instructions.

1 2 . Preheat your iron, with the steam off, to an appropriate heat setting for the interfacing. Take the front tricorder piece and place it facedown on your ironing surface. Lay the rectangle felt piece over the eyelet backs, completely covering the holes. Place the front tricorder interfacing piece over the back of the front tricorder vinyl piece, making sure that the glue side is facedown. Iron carefully. This will keep the piece of felt in place, protect your possessions from getting scratched by the eyelet backs inside the purse, and give some extra stability to the shape.

1 3 . Once it has cooled down, flip the piece over, and use the original front tricorder paper pattern as a placement guide to figure out where the square piece goes. Glue the square piece in place and let it dry according to the manufacturer's instructions.

1 4 . While that is drying, you can work on the back tricorder piece. Take your zipper and fit it into the middle slit, closed zipper tab at the top. Pin it in place on both sides of the zipper. Stitch the zipper ¼ inch in from the vinyl edge.

NOTE: Move the zipper tab to the opposite edge of where you are sewing when needed so your presser foot has room to pass.

1 5. Pin the front tricorder and back tricorder together along the sides and bottom, right sides facing out. Fold the two pieces of nylon webbing in half and place the D rings in the crease. Using the original pattern as a guide, slide these between the front and back pieces so only the D rings and a small amount of nylon webbing stick out. Pin down.

1 6. Sew along the entire outside edges ¼ inch.

1 7. Add a strap to your purse and you're good to go!

PERSONAL LOG

When I was growing up, every Sunday afternoon my family would drive to my grandparents' farm in the country. This was always exciting, as our many cousins and their families would also attend these weekly gatherings. The kids would end the day by watching something on television (my own family watched very little TV, so this was a treat). Nine or ten of the younger cousins, including me, would lie on the broadloom carpet in front of the television in my grandparents' living room and watch reruns of *TOS*. Being young children we thought the wonderful campiness was quite hilarious. One episode in particular, "The Devil in the Dark," has stuck in my mind after all these years. While on a mining colony, the crew of the *Enterprise* encounters a creature called a Horta. The creature was made of molten stone, but my cousins and I deemed it the pizza monster due to its similarities to the bubbling cheese and toppings. I remember us shrieking with laughter at the absurdity of the pizza monster and the jokes that ensued later while eating pizza at other gatherings. For me, *Star Trek* brings forth many great memories such as these; that's why I have been a fan since a young age.

—ASHLEY LOTECKI

4

— TREKKERS IN TRAINING —

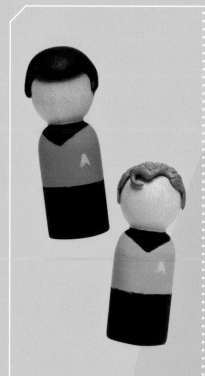

2: MY *STAR TREK* BOOK OF COLORS

3: EMBROIDERED STARFLEET ACADEMY BIB

1: KIRK AND SPOCK PEG PEOPLE

4: COMMANDER SHRAN ANDORIAN RATTLE

5: KHAN FINGER PUPPET

GET YOUR YOUNG ONES STARTED OFF RIGHT WITH THESE KID-FRIENDLY CRAFTS. AFTER JUST A FEW "TRAINING SESSIONS," THEY'LL BE READY FOR THEIR STARFLEET ACADEMY ENTRANCE EXAMS IN NO TIME.

As a military vessel, the *Enterprise* doesn't have a lot of kids running around. Children were generally introduced into the story only to create havoc and unpredictable story lines. Take, for instance, Miri, a teenage girl who lives on a planet that resembles 1960s Earth. In the *TOS* episode that bears her name, the girl develops a crush on Captain Kirk. After becoming jealous of Kirk's attention to Yeoman Janice Rand, Miri enlists the aid of the other children to steal the crew's communicators and kidnap the yeoman.

The children of several of the show's creators and stars guest-starred as "onlies" (because only the children were left when the adults died). William Shatner's daughter Lisabeth is the girl in the red-striped dress.

Keep the children in your life out of trouble (and away from potential robbery and kidnapping charges) with this wooden toy project—or maybe just make yourself something fun to decorate your apartment or work cubicle.

KIRK AND SPOCK PEG PEOPLE BY DIANA PAYNE

INSTRUCTIONS

1. Create a sketch of what you want the figures to look like, defining the outlines of the uniforms. Set aside.

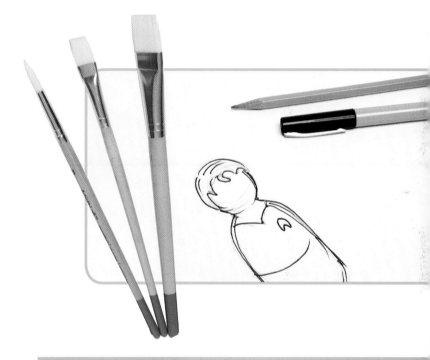

TOOLS & SUPPLIES

- PAPER
- PENCIL
- POLYMER CLAY IN A NEUTRAL COLOR
- WOOD MEN/GAME PIECES
- COOKIE SHEET
- ACRYLIC PAINTS IN BLUE, YELLOW, BLACK, SILVER, BROWN, AND GOLD
- PAINTBRUSHES
- GLUE

NOTE: Invest in a small set of good-quality brushes, as opposed to the ones that come with sets of paint, as these generic-type brushes are very coarse. For this project, a package of four white nylon brushes (two round and two shaders) should work well. You may also want to invest in a fine-pointed brush for the smaller details (like the insignia) to get cleaner lines.

2. Knead the clay for a couple of minutes to make it more pliable.

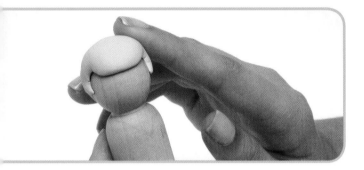

- For Spock, roll some clay into a little ball, push it onto the peg head, and shape his distinctive bowl cut with your fingers. Give his bangs a little curve to make them more realistic. For the sideburns, pinch out and shape the clay in the appropriate places. Check that they are even on both sides.
- For Kirk, roll the clay into small strips and place them onto his head to give his hair a more "combed" look. Using this "strip" method, you can also give him a little side part. Remember that Kirk combs his hair to the right. Take your time forming the hair and you'll be more pleased with your results.

3. With the clay still on the figures, place the wooden men on a cookie sheet and bake according to clay instructions. Keeping the clay on the wood ensures that the clay will hold its shape. This process shouldn't take long, though baking time varies. The particular clay used in the example (Craftsmart polymer clay) instructs to bake the clay at 275 degrees F (135 degrees C) for 15 minutes per ¼-inch thickness. Since the clay on these figures is much thinner than that, your baking time may not be more than 10 minutes.

4. Allow the clay to cool before gently removing it from the peg. This might take a few tries; if the clay doesn't come off at first, let it sit for a few more minutes before trying again.

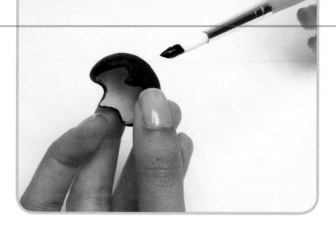

5. Once you've successfully removed the clay, paint the hair piece with acrylic paint. Use a coarse-bristle brush to give the hair some texture with the illusion of individual hairs. You also might want to paint the hair in sections—for example, paint the right side first and let it dry before painting the left. You'll get less paint on your fingers when you hold the hair this way. Set aside to dry.

6. Lightly pencil in some guidelines for when you paint the uniform on the body of your figure so you won't have to guess the boundaries of each paint color. Include guidelines for the collar and insignia.

Trekker TIP!

HAVE A CUP OF WATER AND A PAPER TOWEL NEARBY SO YOU CAN RINSE AND DRY YOUR USED PAINTBRUSHES, ESPECIALLY IF YOU NEED TO USE THE SAME BRUSH FOR A DIFFERENT COLOR.

7. Using a smooth paintbrush, paint the peg bodies with the appropriate colors. To get a crisp, distinct border between the shirt and slacks, wrap a strip of paper or masking tape around the figure as a guide to mark the boundary. Once the first section you paint has dried, use the paper or tape again to help guide you when you paint the second section. Let dry.

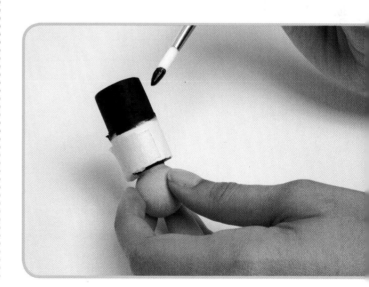

THINNER BRUSHES ARE GREAT TO USE NOT ONLY ON THE INSIGNIA BUT ON THE PART OF THE COLLAR RIGHT ALONG THE NECK AND THE PART WHERE THE BLACK MEETS THE COLOR OF THE SHIRT.

8. **Don't forget to paint the insignia.**

9. Once the paint on both hair and body are dry, glue the hair pieces on the peg heads.

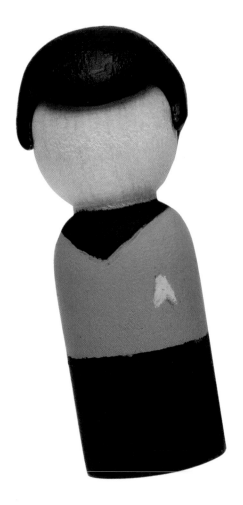

More than any specific *Star Trek* episode or movie, the fans are what makes the franchise so special for me. When you see a spark in a person's eye or hear the excitement in their voice that comes just from saying words like *tribble*, or from seeing someone else wear Spock ears, that in turn makes your day a little more fun. What can be better than a life with more fun?

—JESSICA KARPER

With its wide spectrum of life-forms, diverse planetary flora and fauna, and foods from different cultures, the *Star Trek* universe is colorful. Keeping track of everything is a full-time job for the *Enterprise* database. How hard would it be for an amnesiac to reacquaint herself with this vibrant world?

In the *TOS* episode "The Changeling," the *U.S.S. Enterprise* encounters the space-going computer probe Nomad. The crew beams Nomad aboard, where it promptly erases Uhura's memory. After this attack, McCoy discovers that Uhura's brain is undamaged but she must relearn what the probe erased, including her colors and how to read. Perhaps this book of colors would have helped.

Teach the children in your life their colors with these examples from the *Star Trek* rainbow. Use the templates in the appendix to start, and then add more entries to your book by finding images of different aliens, food, and the like online.

MY *STAR TREK* BOOK OF COLORS
BY ANGIE PEDERSEN

TOOLS & SUPPLIES

- PATTERN PAPER IN VARIOUS COLORS
- SCISSORS
- CHIPBOARD BOOK (EXAMPLE IS 4 INCHES × 6 INCHES, HOLE PUNCHED)
- CARDSTOCK (CARDSTOCK DIE CUTS WITH WINDOW OPENING, OPTIONAL—AVAILABLE IN SCRAPBOOKING STORES) IN VARIOUS COLORS
- X-ACTO KNIFE
- CRAFT GLUE
- PRINTER

INSTRUCTIONS

1. Trim the pattern paper to fit the chipboard page and adhere them together.

2. Fold the cardstock in half to form a flap, and then trim to fit the chipboard page, then cut a window in the front flap (or use precut die cut with window opening). Adhere it to the pattern paper on a chipboard page.

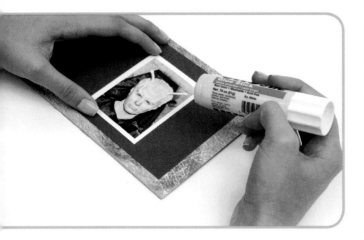

3. Copy or scan the images from the appendix and trim them to size. Adhere each image inside the appropriate color cardstock so it will be revealed when the flap is lifted. Expand your book by searching for additional images—and make sure to choose photos that reflect the colors of cardstock you're using.

4. Type up all of your color words and character names in a word-processing program. Be sure to use a Trekker font!

5. Print and trim your color word piece to size, and then adhere it to the cardstock flap.

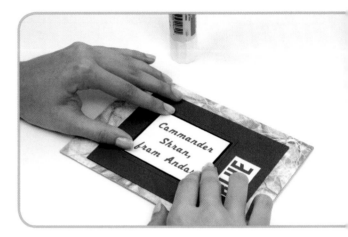

6. Print and trim your character name piece to size, and then adhere it to the cardstock flap.

7. Complete steps 1–5 for each color page.

8. Don't forget your cover! Type up *My Star Trek Book of Colors* in your Trekker font. Print and trim it to size, and use it to create a cover for your board book. Embellish the page with torn pieces of colored cardstock.

Starfleet Academy: where young cadets get their first taste of life in the space-based military. Following a rigorous admission process of exams, the infamous "psych test," and six weeks of summer school, students take classes such as advanced hand-to-hand combat, astrophysics, basic warp design, and stellar cartography. They also complete a battery of training exercises designed to test their leadership mettle.

One such exercise is the *Kobayashi Maru*, known for being a no-win situation—unless you're James Kirk. In the 2009 movie *Star Trek*, Kirk went up against the exercise designed by Spock, and failed twice. With some computer algorithm tweaking and wooing of a certain green-skinned female cadet, Kirk's third attempt was successful, making him the only cadet to ever best the test.

Put your little one on the fast track to command with this decorative yet useful Starfleet Academy bib. This piece incorporates just a few basic embroidery stitches for a truly stellar project.

EMBROIDERED STARFLEET ACADEMY BIB
BY SAMANTHA TOWNSEND

TOOLS & SUPPLIES

- PENCIL
- IRON-ON FUSIBLE WEB (E.G., PELLON WONDER-UNDER)
- SCISSORS
- SCRAPS OF RED AND BLACK FABRIC
- IRON
- YELLOW FABRIC
- TOWELING (OR FLEECE)
- RECOMMENDED: 4-INCH EMBROIDERY HOOP
- FABRIC-MARKING TOOLS (RECOMMENDED: DISAPPEARING INK PEN, WHITE ERASABLE PENCIL, OR REGULAR PENCIL)
- SEWING MACHINE
- EMBROIDERY FLOSS IN RED, BLACK, AND YELLOW
- EMBROIDERY NEEDLE
- VELCRO

INSTRUCTIONS

Use this image for reference as you create the Starfleet logo.

1. Using the patterns in the appendix, trace the appliqué pieces onto the paper side of the fusible web with a sharp pencil. Cut around the traced shapes leaving a good margin.

2. Apply the fusible web to the scraps of black and red fabric by ironing the shiny side of the fusible web to the wrong side of the fabric (follow packaging instructions for best results). Cut out the appliqué shapes.

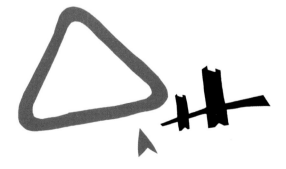

3. Cut out the yellow fabric and the toweling using the pattern in the appendix.

4. Transfer the embroidery pattern markings from the pattern to the yellow fabric, and use a satin stitch to fill the marked spaces. Follow the examples for color and placement.

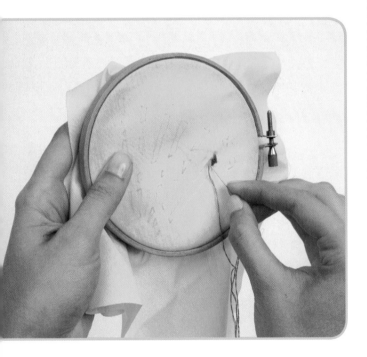

Trekker TIP! PLACE THE YELLOW FABRIC IN AN EMBROIDERY HOOP TO MAKE STITCHING EASIER AND MORE UNIFORM.

5. Peel off the paper backing from the applique shapes and position them within the design, then iron them down to secure.

6. Using the embroidery floss in a straight embroidery stitch, outline the appliqué pieces and add definition to the bridge.

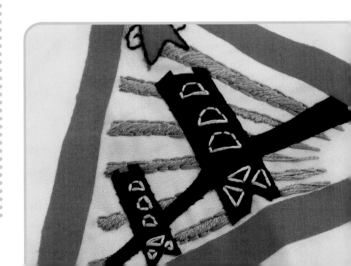

7. With right sides facing each other, use your sewing machine to sew the toweling and yellow fabric together, leaving a hole for turning. There is a ½-inch seam allowance included on the pattern.

8. Turn right side out and iron. Use your sewing machine to topstitch close to the edge of the work.

9. Round off the edges of the Velcro and sew in place.

A blue-skinned, white-haired race from the moon Andor, Andorians usually show up looking for a fight. Militaristic and xenophobic, they generally don't play nice with other races.

One Andorian character, however, proves to be an ally on several occasions. In the *ENT* episode "Babel One," Andorian Commander Shran advises Captain Archer on where to fire on the Andorian ship in order to knock out its shields. And in "The Andorian Incident," Shran and Archer work together to uncover a covert long-range sensor array in a Vulcan monastery. Shran also provides crucial technical and tactical sensor readings that help the *Enterprise* forestall an attack on Earth by the Xindi in "Proving Ground."

Just to show that some Andorians can be cute and cuddly, fire up your sewing machine and crank out an adorable Andorian rattle for a Trekker in Training. For some sound, along with the stuffing add a jingle bell, crinkly cellophane, or dried beans in an old-school film canister.

COMMANDER SHRAN
ANDORIAN RATTLE   BY ANGIE PEDERSEN

CAPTAIN: ▲▲▲

TOOLS & SUPPLIES

- SCISSORS
- RULER OR TAPE MEASURE
- ROTARY CUTTER (OPTIONAL)
- ½ YARD OF FLEECE, LIGHT BLUE
- FELT, BLACK
- FAUX FUR, WHITE
- SEWING MACHINE
- THREAD TO MATCH: LIGHT BLUE, WHITE, AND BLACK
- PENCIL (OPTIONAL)
- FIBERFILL
- JINGLE BELL
- NEEDLE

INSTRUCTIONS

1. Gather supplies and cut material.

From the fleece, cut:
- 6-inch × 8-inch rectangle for the rattle body
- 2 2-inch circles
- 2 1½-inch rectangles for the antennae

From the felt, cut 2 small ovals for eyes.

From the faux fur, cut a 2-inch × 3-inch rectangle for the hair.

2. Fold the body in half lengthwise and sew a seam to create a tube.

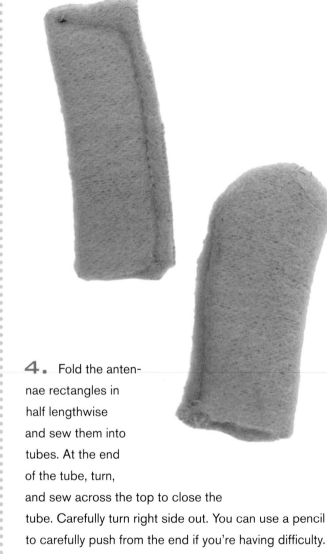

3. Working inside out, sew one fleece circle to one end of the tube. If you have any pen marks on the material, make sure they will not show on the outside once you turn the tube right side out. Sew the second circle to the other end of the tube, but leave a small opening for turning and stuffing. Sewing the circles to the tube can be tricky—go slowly and make sure you catch both layers in the seam.

4. Fold the antennae rectangles in half lengthwise and sew them into tubes. At the end of the tube, turn, and sew across the top to close the tube. Carefully turn right side out. You can use a pencil to carefully push from the end if you're having difficulty.

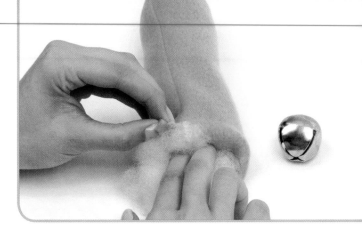

5. Turn the body right side out and stuff with fiberfill. Include a bell or other noisemaker in the middle of the stuffing. Hand-stitch the top opening closed. Don't worry too much about your stitches; you can hide them with the hair.

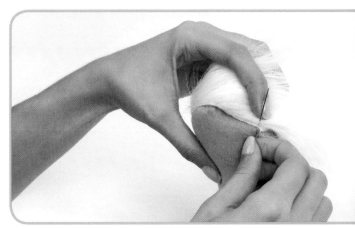

6. Hand-stitch on the fur/hair, antennae, and felt eyes.

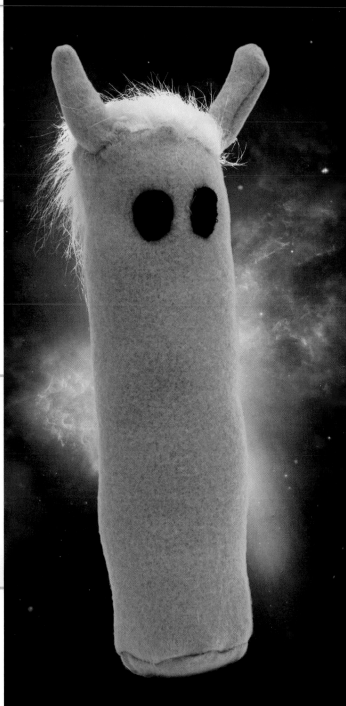

One of the most notorious villains in the *Star Trek* universe, Khan Noonien Singh led a group of genetically engineered "super humans" with enhanced physical strength and analytical capabilities. Khan ruled over about one-quarter of Earth's population. Forced from power during the late-twentieth-century Eugenics Wars, he and eighty-four followers escaped aboard the *S.S. Botany Bay*.

After drifting through space for over two centuries, Khan encountered Captain Kirk and crew in the *TOS* episode "Space Seed." Khan tried to take over the *Enterprise* but was thwarted and left with his group on Ceti Alpha V. The crew met Khan again in *Star Trek II: The Wrath of Khan* while searching for a test site for Project Genesis. Khan's bitterness toward Kirk led to an epic battle, ultimately ending in Khan's defeat.

Though the puppet's pectorals aren't quite as impressive as the live specimen's, you can still have fun ruling over your own little piece of the cosmos with this project.

KHAN FINGER PUPPET

BY HEATHER MANN

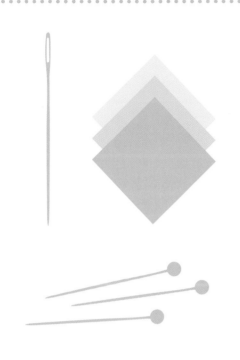

TOOLS & SUPPLIES

- SCISSORS
- FELT SHEETS IN ORANGE, GOLDEN BROWN, BEIGE, BLACK, AND GRAY
- TACKY CRAFT GLUE
- BLACK EMBROIDERY FLOSS
- EMBROIDERY NEEDLE
- RULER OR TAPE MEASURE
- MARABOU TRIM IN WHITE
- PINS OR SMALL BINDER CLIPS
- 2 GOOGLY EYES

INSTRUCTIONS

1 .   Using the pattern in the appendix, cut out the pattern pieces.

2 .   Glue the costume pieces to the front of the body in this order: shirt front, collar pieces, pants, belt, and belt buckle.

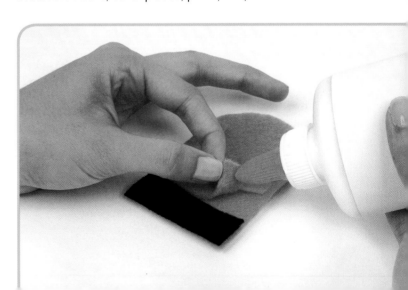

3. Embroider eyebrows with embroidery floss.

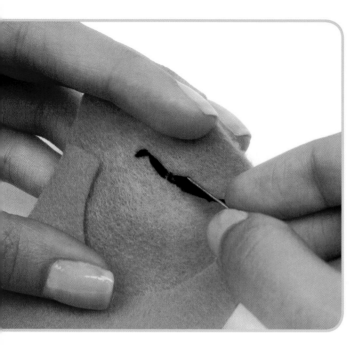

4. Cut a piece of black embroidery floss about 18 inches long. Divide it into three strands and knot it at one end. Add embroidery lines on the collar and a graduated zigzag on the buckle.

5. Glue the shirt back to the back body piece.

6. Place front and back puppet pieces together facing each other.

7. Cut a 4-inch piece of marabou trim and sandwich it between the front and back pieces around the head. Most of the trim should be inside the puppet, but some of it should be sticking out around the edges. Pin the pieces together.

8. With embroidery floss and needle, sew around the sides and top of the puppet, leaving the bottom open. You should catch some of the marabou trim in the seam as you sew. (Whipstitching is the easiest way to make sure the marabou is secure!)

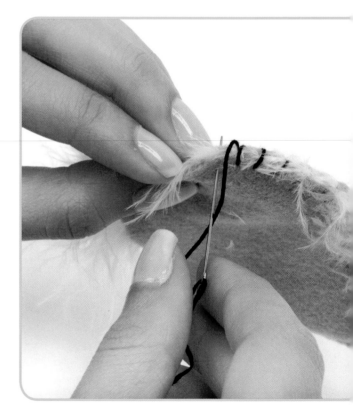

9. Gently turn the finger puppet right side out. Fluff Khan's hair.

10. Glue on the googly eyes.

11. Cut a ¾-inch piece of marabou trim for his bangs, and glue on. Allow the glue to dry. Give Khan a little trim on his bangs—straight across.

5

— SET YOUR PHASERS TO PARTY —

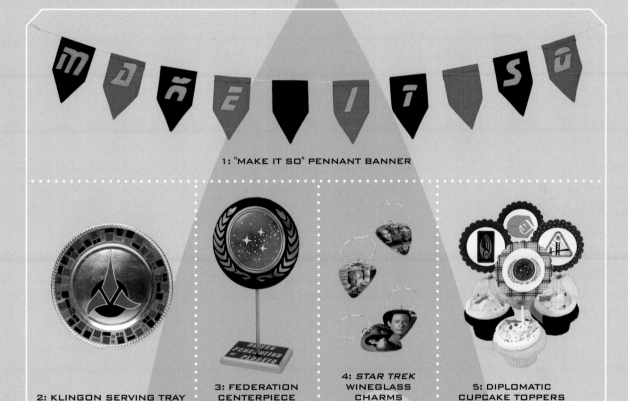

1: "MAKE IT SO" PENNANT BANNER

2: KLINGON SERVING TRAY

3: FEDERATION CENTERPIECE

4: *STAR TREK* WINEGLASS CHARMS

5: DIPLOMATIC CUPCAKE TOPPERS

FROM ROOM DECORATIONS TO JUST THE RIGHT TOUCH FOR YOUR TABLE, HERE ARE A FEW PROJECTS THAT WILL SPRUCE UP YOUR NEXT INFORMAL GATHERING OF YOUR FAVORITE GEEKS. THESE PROJECTS WILL MAKE SURE YOUR PARTY IS STELLAR!

M ake it so" is one of Captain Jean-Luc Picard's catchphrases on *TNG*. Perhaps it's actor Patrick Stewart's knighthood and background in Shakespearean acting that makes the line delivery seem so compelling. While quietly commanding as a captain, he brooks no argument and expects his orders to be carried out to the letter.

Often when the *Enterprise* faces a challenge, Picard gathers his senior officers in his briefing room to offer insights and opinions. Ever the diplomat, he listens to all input and then decides a course of action, decreeing that they go forward and "make it so." Commands to his first officer, William Riker, have the addition of "Number One."

Channel your inner Picard with this pennant banner and let your party guests know that they are hereby commanded to have a good time at your gathering. Picard would want them to enjoy themselves, and who are they to argue with the captain?

"MAKE IT SO" PENNANT BANNER BY JORDAN ELLIS

 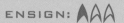

TOOLS & SUPPLIES

- IRON
- 50-INCH × 8-INCH PIECE OF 100% COTTON/BROADCLOTH FABRIC, BLACK
- PENCIL
- MARKER
- 50-INCH × 8-INCH PIECE OF 100% COTTON/BROADCLOTH FABRIC, RED
- SCISSORS
- 8 STANDARD-SIZE PIECES FELT, GRAY OR SILVER
- FUSIBLE WEB OR FABRIC GLUE (OPTIONAL)
- THREAD TO MATCH FABRICS AND FELT
- NEEDLE
- PINS
- SEWING MACHINE
- SAFETY PIN
- 6 FEET OF CORDING (E.G., HEMP, COTTON ROPE)

INSTRUCTIONS

1. Iron your fabric. Using the pattern in the appendix, trace the pennant triangle 10 times each on the black and red fabric (20 pieces total). Cut out all of the pieces.

2. Using the letter patterns in the appendix, trace each of the letters onto the felt and cut them out.

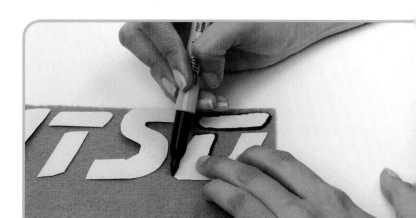

3. Line up 10 of the fabric triangles in alternating colors (black, red, black, etc.). Place one felt letter in the center of each triangle, spelling out "Make It So." Leave a blank triangle between each word.

4. Attach the felt letters to the fabric with hand-stitching, fusible web, or fabric glue.

5. When all of the letters are attached, place a second fabric triangle of the same color on top, right sides of the fabric together. Pin around the edges.

6. Sew with a ¼-inch seam allowance around the two sides of the triangle, leaving the top open. Flip the pennant inside out so the letters are on the outside. Iron it flat.

7. Fold the top of the pennant over to the back side. Stitch or glue along the bottom edge to make a tube for the hanging cord.

9. Tie a loop in each end of the cording to make hanging easier, and it's ready to join your party!

8. Attach a safety pin to one end of the cord and push the cord through the tube at the top of each pennant piece. Remember to keep the pennants in order so they spell out the words correctly.

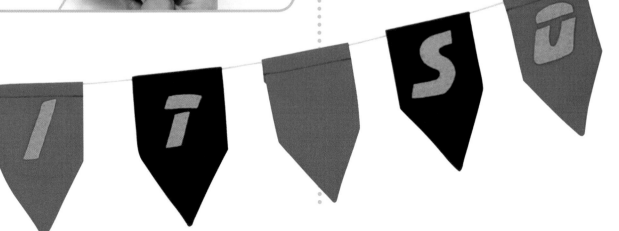

Join a group of warlike Klingons for dinner at your own risk: One offhanded comment could pit you in a battle to the death with *bat'leths* (meaning "swords of honor," traditional Klingon crescent-shaped blade weapons). But Commander William Riker is not one to shy away from a challenge. In the *TNG* episode "A Matter of Honor," Riker volunteers to participate in the Starfleet Officer Exchange Program and serve upon the Klingon warship the *Pagh*. In one scene, Riker joins the crew for a meal, dining on such Klingon delicacies as *gagh* (live bloodworms), *bregit lung*, and *rokeg* blood pie. In addition to the distinctive fare, Riker endures lustful looks from the female Klingons and some generally good-natured ribbing from the crew.

Riker's meal might have been served on a platter much like this one. Klingons are fond of sturdy tableware with some heft to it, meant to take a beating (because it very well might).

KLINGON SERVING TRAY

BY ANGIE PEDERSEN

ENSIGN: ΛΛΛ

TOOLS & SUPPLIES

- CARDSTOCK IN RED AND BLACK
- PENCIL
- SCISSORS
- SMALL PAINTBRUSH
- DECOUPAGE GLUE (E.G., MOD PODGE)
- PLASTIC SERVING PLATTER IN SILVER
- SQUARE AND RECTANGLE PAPER PUNCHES
- A SELECTION OF PATTERN PAPER IN REDS AND BLACKS

INSTRUCTIONS

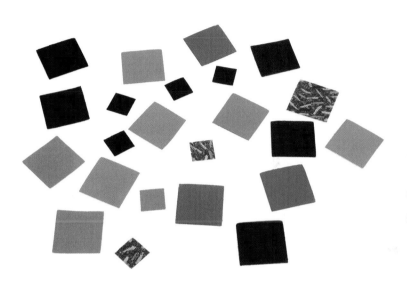

1. Copy and cut out the Klingon symbol and black circle. Adhere them to cardstock and trim.

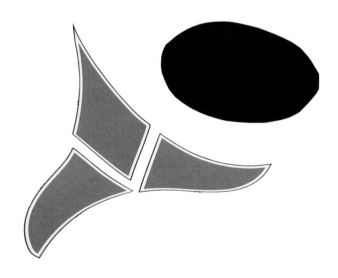

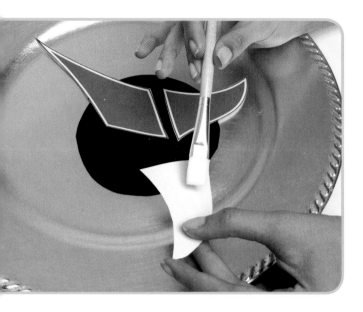

2. Using the small paintbrush, brush Mod Podge onto the back of the black circle and adhere it to the center of the plate. Brush Mod Podge onto the back of each piece of the Klingon symbol and adhere on top of black circle. Smooth out pieces to remove any wrinkles or air pockets. Once smoothed down, brush Mod Podge on top of the symbol and circle to seal. Let dry.

3. Using paper punches, punch out squares and rectangles from the pattern paper and leftover card-stock. Place the pieces in a mosaic pattern around edge of plate to give yourself an idea of how many punched pieces you'll need to complete the design.

4. Using the small paintbrush, brush Mod Podge onto the backs of the punched pieces and adhere them around edge of plate. Once all pieces are adhered, brush Mod Podge on top to seal. Let dry.

NOTE: This project cannot get wet and should not be washed either by hand or in the dishwasher. Use it to serve dry foods like bread or rolls, chips, or individually wrapped snacks like cupcakes.
Wipe clean with a dry cloth.

The United Federation of Planets, commonly referred to as the Federation, is a sort of interstellar United Nations composed of planetary governments that have agreed to exist under a single central government. Founded on the principles of universal liberty, rights, and equality, the Federation seeks to share knowledge and resources in peaceful cooperation and space exploration. It formed Starfleet to fulfill exploratory, scientific, diplomatic, and defense functions.

Though it's in all the other series, the Federation does not appear in *ENT*, because the series is set prior to its formation. However, in the episode "United," set in 2154, Captain Archer helps form a preliminary alliance among Humans, Vulcans, Andorians, and Tellarites—the four species that eventually form the Federation in 2161.

Invoke the solemn dignity of the Federation at your next gathering with this centerpiece. Use it as a talisman of good will for your party, then later as an interstellar paperweight.

FEDERATION CENTERPIECE

BY DAVID CHEANEY

TOOLS & SUPPLIES

- CHIPBOARD/CARDBOARD BOX, CIRCULAR WITH LID
- PENCIL
- SHARP CRAFT BLADE
- GLUE
- PINEWOOD PLAQUE
- $5/16$-INCH DOWEL CUT TO LENGTH
- FOAM PAINTBRUSH
- SPRAY PAINT, GOLD
- SCISSORS
- TWO PRINTOUTS OF THE FEDERATION LOGO IMAGE
- ONE PRINTOUT OF THE FEDERATION LABEL
- DECOUPAGE GLUE (E.G., MOD PODGE
- DRILL AND $5/16$-INCH DRILL BIT

INSTRUCTIONS

1. Take the lid from the box, fit it over the bottom of the box, and use your pencil to draw a cut line around the bottom of the box.

2. Using the craft blade, cut around the bottom of the box until you have two separate pieces (the original top of the box and the bottom) that fit together. Glue the two pieces together so that you have a two-sided disk.

3. Spray-paint the edges of the disk, dowel, and wood plaque gold.

UNITED FEDERATION OF PLANETS

4. Cut out the Federation graphics to fit on either side of the disc and Mod Podge them into place, gently smoothing out wrinkles with your fingertips or the edge of an old credit card. Trim the Federation label to fit on the wooden plaque base. Mod Podge the label onto the base, smoothing out wrinkles.

5. Mark the center of the wood plaque and drill a hole. Drill another hole in the bottom of the disk. Glue the dowel into the base and into the bottom of the disk.

W alk into any bar on a Federation out-
post, and you're sure to find a bevy of
beverages to choose from, including a
wide variety of alcoholic drinks.

Quark is known to stock the shelves of
his bar on Deep Space 9 with Saurian brandy.
In "The Trouble with Tribbles," Chief Engineer
Montgomery Scott enjoys a "wee bit" of traditional Scotch whisky.

In *Star Trek II: The Wrath of Khan*, McCoy
gives Kirk a bottle of outlawed Romulan
ale. Kirk also serves Romulan ale at a state
dinner with Klingons in *Star Trek VI: The
Undiscovered Country*, but after the ensu-
ing hangover, he creates a Captain's Log to
remind him never to serve it at diplomatic
functions again.

These inventive and reusable wineglass
charms will help keep track of your drink in
Star Trek style.

STAR TREK WINEGLASS
CHARMS BY JESSICA COMPEL

ENSIGN: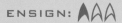

TOOLS & SUPPLIES

- ASSORTED *STAR TREK* IMAGES (FAN MAGAZINES ARE A GREAT SOURCE FOR THESE)
- GUITAR PICKS (CRAFT STORES SELL PACKS OF 12 PLASTIC PICKS WITH PREDRILLED HOLES)
- PENCIL OR PEN
- EMBROIDERY SCISSORS OR OTHER SHARP, POINTED SCISSORS FOR DETAIL CUTTING
- GLASS AND BEAD GLUE FOR SLICK SURFACES
- TOOTHPICKS
- PAPER TOWELS FOR CLEANUP
- STRAIGHT PIN
- 6-MILLIMETER JUMP RINGS
- JEWELRY PLIERS
- SMALL, FLAT PAINTBRUSH
- DECOUPAGE GLUE (E.G., MOD PODGE), CLASSIC GLOSS-LUSTER FINISH
- WINEGLASS CHARM HOOPS (FOUND AT CRAFT STORES, OR YOU CAN ORDER THEM FROM ETSY SUPPLIERS)

INSTRUCTIONS

1. Decide how many charms you want to make. A standard set of wineglasses contains six glasses.

2. Choose your images. Have a guitar pick handy to test the size of your images.

Trekker TIP!

FAN MAGAZINES ARE A GREAT SOURCE OF IMAGES FOR YOUR WINEGLASS CHARMS, AND YOU CAN FIND VINTAGE *STAR TREK* FAN MAGAZINES IN ONLINE BULK SALES. THIS IS A GREAT WAY TO STOCKPILE PICTURES FOR FUTURE PROJECTS.

3. Place your first guitar pick on top of the picture and trace around it. Cut out your image on the trace line using small sharp scissors.

4. Squeeze a small amount (about the size of a pea) of glass and bead glue onto the pick. Gently spread the glue around with a toothpick. Next place your picture on the guitar pick and position it to cover the entire pick. Press your picture down and wipe off the edges where any glue seeped out.

5. Looking at the back of the guitar pick, use sharp scissors to trim the edges of the picture to fit the pick.

6. Poke a hole through the picture with the straight pin, using the predrilled hole in the guitar pick for placement.

7. Repeat steps 3 through 6 for remaining wine-glass charms.

8. Allow all the guitar picks to dry overnight.

9. Add a jump ring through all the dried guitar picks. Use the mini jeweler's pliers to open the jump ring, feed the jump ring through the hole in the guitar pick and picture, then close the jump ring with the pliers.

10. Use a small, flat paintbrush to apply a thin, even coat of Mod Podge over the image. Use the tip of your brush to apply under and around the jump ring. Repeat this step for each guitar pick. Allow to dry for 20 minutes.

11. Add a wineglass charm hoop to each guitar pick through the jump rings.

As members of Starfleet, the crew of the *Enterprise* often have to host diplomatic gatherings, so they are well versed in how to interact with those from different cultures. Not so for the omnipotent species of the Q continuum. In the *VOY* episode "Q2," Q leaves his son Junior on *Voyager* to learn some manners and respect. In an effort to help teach Junior about diplomacy, Chakotay devises a holodeck program where Junior must settle a mining dispute among a Bajoran, a Bolian, a Cardassian, a Ferengi, a Nausicaan, and a Romulan. Let's just say Junior doesn't learn his lesson.

You'll have better luck with your own "diplomatic" gathering—especially if you serve cupcakes. These cupcake toppers represent a variety of cultures and organizations: the Romulan Star Empire, the Borg collective, the Ferengi Alliance, Starfleet Command, Starfleet Academy, and the United Federation of Planets.

DIPLOMATIC CUPCAKE TOPPERS
BY ANGIE PEDERSEN

INSTRUCTIONS

1. Copy or scan and print the images in the appendix onto cardstock, about 2 inches tall and wide. You can also make color copies onto cardstock.

2. Using the circle punch, punch out the images.

3. Using the scalloped circle punch, punch out circles from the colored/patterned cardstock.

TOOLS & SUPPLIES

- CARDSTOCK, WHITE
- 2½-INCH ("SUPER") CIRCLE PUNCH
- CARDSTOCK, YOUR CHOICE OF COLOR AND/OR PATTERN
- 3½-INCH ("GIANT") SCALLOPED CIRCLE PUNCH
- ADHESIVE FOAM, SUCH AS POP DOTS
- HOT GLUE GUN AND GLUE STICKS
- LOLLIPOP OR CAKE POP STICKS
- RIBBON

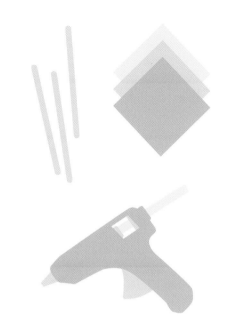

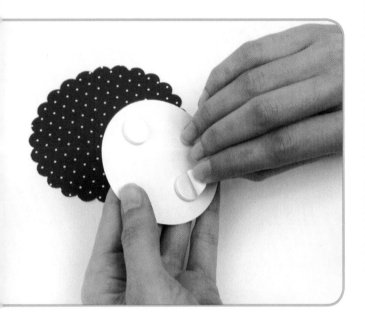

5. Using the hot glue gun, attach the lollipop sticks to the back of the scalloped circles.

4. Using the adhesive foam, attach the smaller circles to the scalloped circles.

6. Tie pieces of ribbon to the sticks.

7. Carefully stick toppers into frosted cupcakes.

AFTERWORD

By now, you are probably aware that I love everything geek, as well as everything craft. But beyond my own need to be creative, I also love to share what I make and other crafty treasures that I find. For me, that's what this book is about.

In 2010 (an apt year, given its sci-fi link), I began blogging for GeekCrafts, which provides its readers a source of crafting ideas based on popular science fiction and fantasy concepts. For me, it's the perfect marriage of geek and craft, and the ideal outlet for me to share inspired ideas so others can craft to their geeky heart's content.

It's also what brought this book project to me. When I was contacted to write a book on *Star Trek* crafts, I felt like I was in the middle of a holodeck scene—like it wasn't completely real. After getting over my initial shock, I jumped at the chance to work on this project. But I admit, I had some reservations.

Every Trekker I know sees *Star Trek* as more than a TV show, more than movies and books. It's about a vision of a future where a galaxy of races can all get along, where peace is possible and poverty is in the past. Trekkers believe in the vision that Gene Roddenberry introduced in 1966. So many people have fond memories of those ideologies. I wanted to create a resource that would stay true to those ideals; I didn't take that responsibility lightly.

My concern was the quality and attention to detail that Trekkers would expect. The TV show and movie sets and props reflect the love that writers, directors, and producers have for the *Star Trek* vision. Think of the finely crafted details like the ornate wooden doors of Ten-Forward in *TNG*, the creative icons like the Vulcan IDIC, or the realistic props like phasers and tricorders. Crafty Trekkers want to create their own version of those items to help demonstrate that aspect of their interests and personalities. Creating these iconic devices helps declare the ideals they hold dear.

Beyond T-shirt costumes and cardboard phasers, I wanted to include projects that crafters would find fun and challenging, while still maintaining the link to all that *Star Trek* stands for in their minds. While I had ideas for crafts that I could create on my own, I also needed to find skilled crafters willing to rise to the challenge.

I spent months combing the Web for the perfect *Star Trek*–related crafts, then contacting designers to participate in this book. Contributors not only needed to provide a finished project, but also materials to illustrate each of the steps in their process of creating the craft. I was asking for time and resources, and a lot of both.

Some crafters I contacted were unable to participate, and it was a disappointment each time someone had to pass on sharing their project. Fortunately, with a little begging, I was able to put together a team of great crafters who shared not only their talents, but their love of *Trek*.

You will find that almost every contributor has a URL listed in the bio section. I highly encourage you to seek them out on the Web. The project each of them shares in this book is only one of their many creative ideas, and you won't be disappointed by their other creations.

After several months, hundreds of e-mails, hours at the post office, and several unexpected scheduling challenges, we, as a team, are proud to bring you this book. I don't believe this book is the end-all crafting book for *Star Trek*. I would like to think that this is just the beginning of what imagination can inspire when creating *Star Trek*–inspired crafts!

Ambassador Sarek aboard the *U.S.S. Enterprise*-D in "Sarek" (*TNG*).

ACKNOWLEDGEMENTS

First I must recognize my contributors—they went out of their way to help with all the step-outs and materials, and sometimes on short deadlines. Thanks so much to Fina Cardwell, David Cheaney, Jessica Compel, Mary Czerwinski, Sarah Dunn, Jordan Ellis, Tara Fields, Hope Furno, Ashley Lotecki, Heather Mann, Shove Mink, Diana Payne, Katie Smith, and Samantha Townsend.

Thanks to Shayne Rioux for inviting me to join the GeekCrafts crew—not only do I love geeking out for my weekly posts, but also I wouldn't have been "found" for this project without my work there!

Thank you to my editor, Leah Jenness, for choosing me for this project, and for all her guidance and patience along the way.

A big thank-you to my family—to my kids, James and Joanne, for their unfailing enthusiasm for my crafting projects (even the craft fails); to my in-laws, John and Sally, for their support and for raising such a *Trek*-savvy son; and definitely to my husband, David, my source for all things *Trek*, for finding the words when I couldn't.

And finally a thank-you to my parents, for always believing in me and encouraging me, and specifically to my dad, for introducing me to *Star Trek* in the first place.

Picard is assimilated into Locutus, who plans to help the Borg assimilate Earth, in "Best of Both Worlds, Part II" (*TNG*).

APPENDIX

"GO BOLDLY" CANVAS

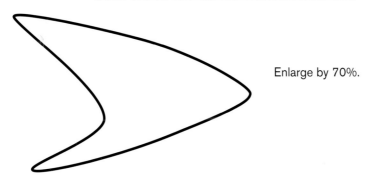

Enlarge by 70%.

"INFINITE DIVERSITY IN INFINITE COMBINATIONS" ENVELOPE-STYLE PILLOWCASE

Enlarge by 70%.

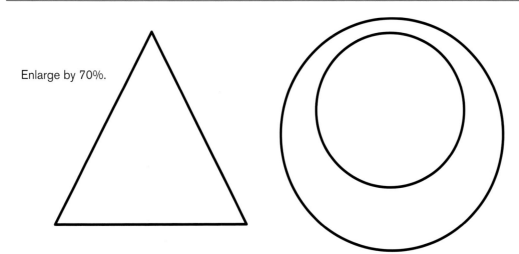

CAPTAIN JAMES T. KIRK
STYLIZED FUSE BEAD FORM

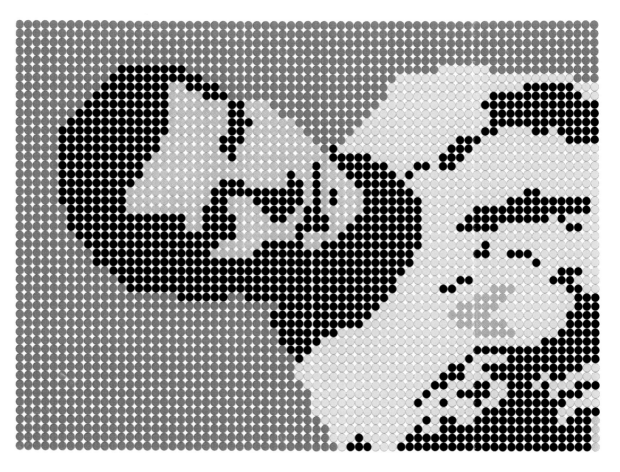

Enlarge by 60%.

STAR TREK: THE ANIMATED SERIES COASTERS

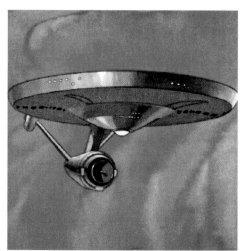

Enlarge by 40%.

U.S.S. ENTERPRISE GLASS BLOCK DECORATION

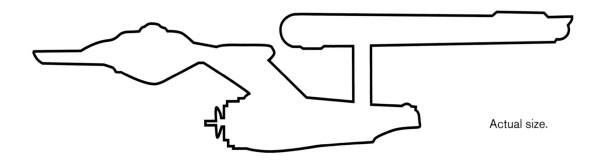

Actual size.

TRIBBLES

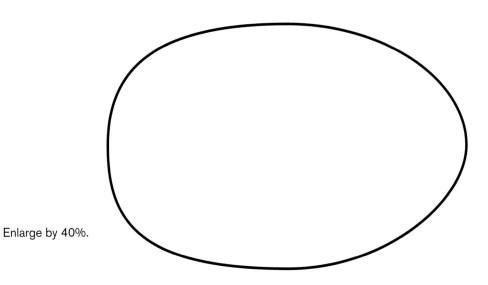

Enlarge by 40%.

SPOCK MONKEY

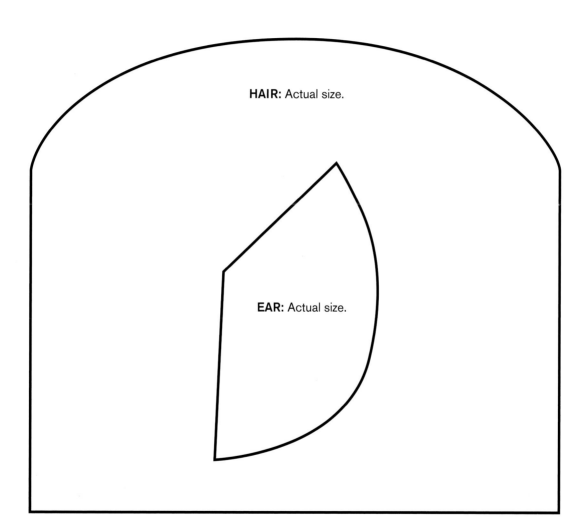

HAIR: Actual size.

EAR: Actual size.

SPOCK MONKEY

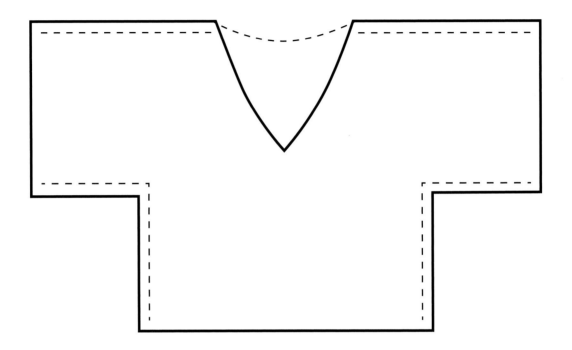

SHIRT: Enlarge by 50%.

INSIGNIA: Actual size.

STAR TREK REVERSIBLE DOG VEST

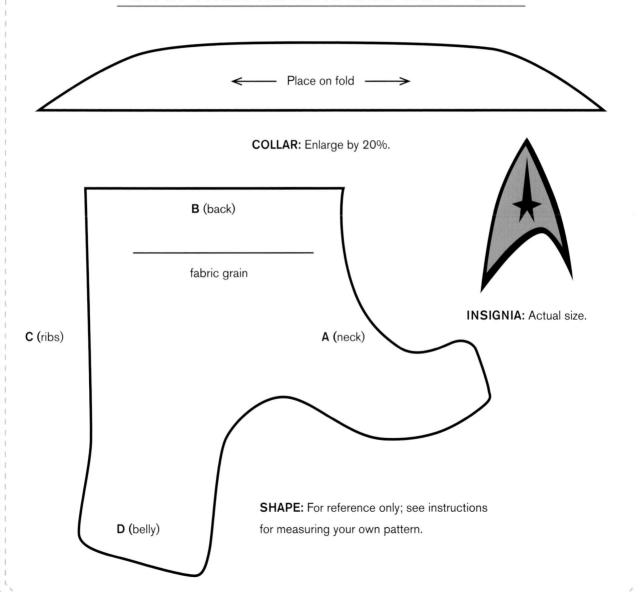

← Place on fold →

COLLAR: Enlarge by 20%.

B (back)

fabric grain

C (ribs)

A (neck)

INSIGNIA: Actual size.

D (belly)

SHAPE: For reference only; see instructions for measuring your own pattern.

CAPTAIN KIRK UNIFORM–INSPIRED GADGET CASE

BACK: Enlarge by 50%. Cut one.

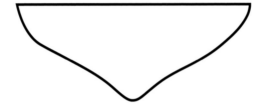

NECK: Enlarge by 50%. Cut one.

DELTA: Enlarge by 50%. Cut one.

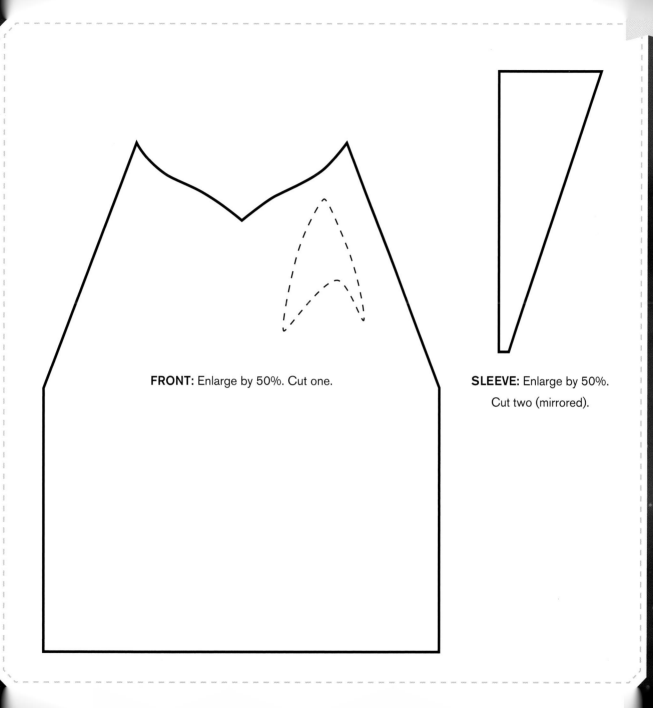

FRONT: Enlarge by 50%. Cut one.

SLEEVE: Enlarge by 50%.

Cut two (mirrored).

STARFLEET UNIFORM APRON

DELTA: Enlarge by 50%.

TRICORDER PURSE

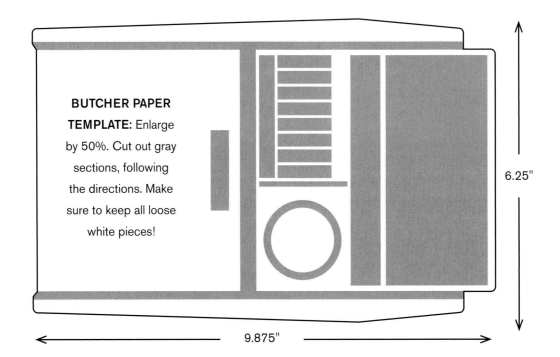

BUTCHER PAPER TEMPLATE: Enlarge by 50%. Cut out gray sections, following the directions. Make sure to keep all loose white pieces!

6.25"

9.875"

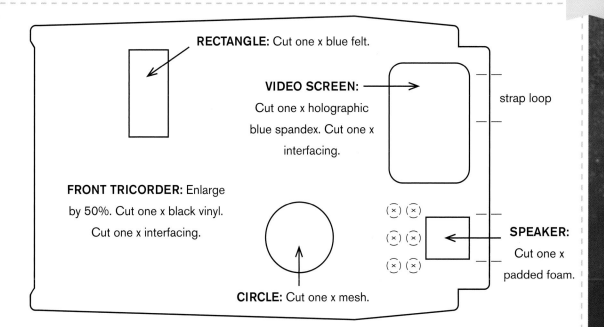

RECTANGLE: Cut one x blue felt.

VIDEO SCREEN: Cut one x holographic blue spandex. Cut one x interfacing.

strap loop

FRONT TRICORDER: Enlarge by 50%. Cut one x black vinyl. Cut one x interfacing.

SPEAKER: Cut one x padded foam.

CIRCLE: Cut one x mesh.

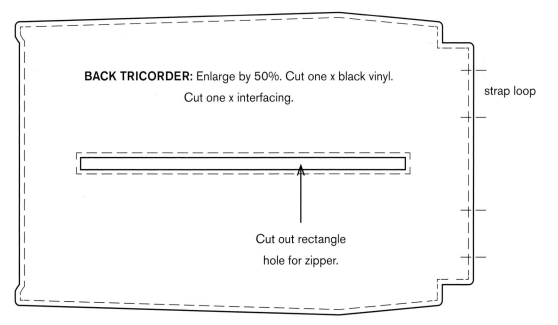

BACK TRICORDER: Enlarge by 50%. Cut one x black vinyl. Cut one x interfacing.

strap loop

Cut out rectangle hole for zipper.

MY *STAR TREK* BOOK OF COLORS

Enlarge by 30%.

EMBROIDERED STARFLEET ACADEMY BIB

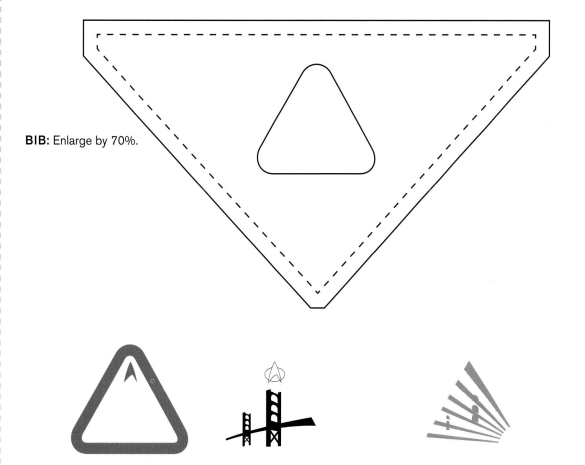

BIB: Enlarge by 70%.

APPLIQUÉ PATTERNS: Enlarge by 70%.

EMROIDERY PATTERN: Enlarge by 70%.

KHAN FINGER PUPPET

ALL PATTERN PIECES: Enlarge by 30%.

SHIRT BACK: Cut one.

SHIRT FRONT: Cut one.

COLLAR PIECES: Cut one each.

BODY: Cut two, one beige (front), one gray (back).

PANTS: Cut one.

BELT: Cut one.

BELT: Cut one.

"MAKE IT SO" PENNANT BANNER

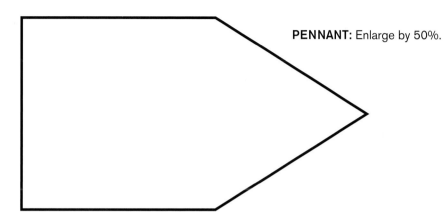

PENNANT: Enlarge by 50%.

LETTERS: Enlarge by 50%.

KLINGON SERVING TRAY

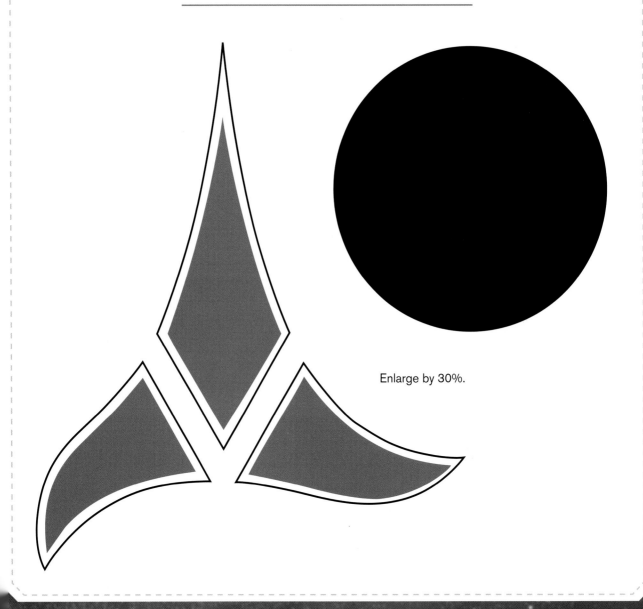

Enlarge by 30%.

FEDERATION CENTERPIECE

Enlarge by 50%; print 2.

FEDERATION CENTERPIECE

UNITED

FEDERATION

OF PLANETS

Actual size.

DIPLOMATIC CUPCAKE TOPPERS

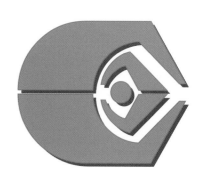

GLOSSARY OF TERMS & TECHNIQUES

Here is a quick guide to some of the crafting techniques and terms used in this book.

CROCHET STITCHES

chain (ch): Start with a loop on your crochet hook. Wrap yarn around your hook ("yarn over"), and pull a loop of yarn through the loop on your hook.

half-double crochet (HDC): Yarn over, insert your crochet hook into the top of next stitch, yarn over, and pull one loop through the stitch. Yarn over again and pull a loop through all three loops on your hook.

single crochet (sc): Insert your crochet hook into the top of a stitch, yarn over, and pull one loop through the stitch. Yarn over again, and pull a loop through both loops on your hook.

slip stitch (sl st): Insert your hook into a stitch, yarn over, and pull a loop through both the stitch and the loop on your hook.

single decrease stitch (dec): Insert your hook into a stitch, yarn over, and pull a loop through the stitch. Keeping both loops on the hook, insert your needle into the next stitch, yarn over, and pull a loop through that second stitch. Then yarn over and pull a loop through all three loops on your hook.

increase stitch (inc): Stitch two stitches into one stitch.

magic ring: Also referred to as a magic circle or magic loop, a magic ring is a way to begin crocheting in the round by crocheting over an adjustable loop, and then pulling the loop tight. It helps keep the work tightly together rather than leaving a hole. For a photo tutorial, visit June Gilbank's tutorial at http://www.planetjune.com /blog/tutorials/magic-ring-right-handed/.

Trekker TIP! WATCH CROCHET GEEK'S VIDEO TUTORIALS ON YOUTUBE TO IMPROVE YOUR CROCHET SKILLS.

DECOUPAGE

This is the act of adhering paper or fabric to a hard surface like wood. First brush a thick glue, like Mod Podge, on the base surface, then brush glue on the back of the paper or fabric. Then apply the paper or fabric to the base surface, making sure to smooth out any bubbles or wrinkles. Once smooth, brush on another layer of glue over the surface of the project to seal it.

EMBROIDERY & HAND-SEWING STITCHES

satin stitch: A series of flat stitches that are used to completely cover a section of the background fabric.

straight stitch: A stitch that passes through the fabric in a simple up and down motion, and generally in a single direction.

whipstitch: A hand-sewing technique used to join two pieces of material together. Place pieces with right sides together, and hold the pieces with the two edges facing up toward you. Secure the thread on the wrong side of one piece. Pass the sewing needle through both pieces of fabric from back to front to start the seam. Move the needle to the left, pass the needle through pieces, again from back to front, wrapping the seam edge with the stitch. Repeat stitches until you have seamed the entire side of fabric pieces together.

SEWING TERMS

fusible web or iron-on adhesive: This product adds stability to a thin fabric and can also act as an adhesive between two pieces of fabric. To apply, cut fusible web to the shape and size needed for pattern. Place the rough side of the fusible webs onto the wrong side of the material to be bonded. Using a no-steam setting on your iron, press with medium pressure for 10–15 seconds. Repeat until the entire surface is bonded. Allow pieces to cool, then check to make sure the fabric is adhered. Remove paper backing, and repeat to adhere to another piece of fabric. Follow manufacturer's instructions for best results.

notch and clip: To make sewn curves and corners lie flat, you can cut out small notches from fabric above the seam of a curve or clip the squared edges from corners. Plenty of tutorials can be found online to help you with your notching and clipping techniques.

right side: The side of the material that is usually displayed outwardly, such as the patterned side.

wrong side: The back side that is usually kept toward the inside.

ABOUT THE CONTRIBUTORS

Fina Cardwell is a crafty mom of three who has interests in sewing, crochet, knitting, embroidery, photography, astronomy, cooking, reading, and computers. She makes her home in Texas and likes to hunt and fish with her husband.

David Cheaney has been a fan of *Star Trek* since he first turned on a TV (which was a looong time ago). After years of trying to figure out what to do with his life, he finally realized that "making stuff" gave him true satisfaction. David now happily refinishes old furniture in his garage and runs an online Etsy shop selling his coasters and other home goods (www.cheltenhamroad .etsy.com). You can follow the adventures of this "reluctant crafter" via his blog at www .cheltenhamroad.wordpress.com.

Jessica Compel received her bachelor of fine arts from Carlow University in Pittsburgh, Pennsylvania. Her craft ideas usually stem from the things she loves: anything geeky, sci-fi, fantasy, Halloween, or fall-related; good books; and great coffee. She sells the items she makes at

Cons and flea markets, and on Etsy at www .etsy.com/shop/rememberthatline. She lives in Pittsburgh with her supportive husband, who doesn't mind the constant buying of craft supplies or bits of beads and yarn lying all over the house. They have six crazy "kids" in the form of five cats and one hermit crab.

Mary Czerwinski is the cohost of *Glue Guns and Phasers*, a *Star Trek* crafting Web series and convention workshop. She also hosts and produces *DVD Geeks*, a DVD review show. As a journalist and crafter, Mary has appeared at various *Star Trek* conventions as a moderator and panelist for StarTrek.com and TrekMovie.com. She currently collaborates with Roddenberry Productions as an interviewer and archivist of *Star Trek* luminaries. You can find her work at www.gluegunsandphasers.blogspot.com or on Etsy at SevenofNineDesign.

Sarah Dunn is originally from Chicago and has always been creative and crafty. She studied at Columbia College Chicago and the Fashion Institute of Design and Merchandising LA, graduating with a degree in fashion design. Sarah started her company, My Geeky Boyfriend, inspired by her real-life geeky boyfriend, when he asked her to make him a set of geek-themed pillowcases. She currently resides in Los Angeles.

Jordan Ellis is a matchmaker of sorts, first introducing and later marrying practicality and pop culture. This Brooklyn-based seamstress creates everything from *Star Trek* aprons to crayon bandoliers in her somewhat cramped, fabric-full studio apartment. Her work is a pitch-perfect fusion of geeky, gritty, and all that is trendy.

TheMistressT, aka **Tara Fields**, is a decorative painter by day and a crafter of various media by night. Recently relocated from Portland, Oregon, to Florence, Montana, she enjoys the mountain life with TheManFlesh and their two dogs, Betty and Delia. Her mottoes include "I'm so glamorous, I cry glitter tears," "There is no such thing as too much carpincho," and "If you wear enough sequins, all you have to do is stand there." She blogs about her adjustment to mountain life at SuddenlyTaxidermy.blogspot.com, and her wares are available at bubbleoffplumb.etsy.com and GreatBigBeautifulDog.etsy.com.

Hope Furno is a teenager who still has the imagination of a five-year-old. Totally addicted to both knitting and crocheting, she also loves books and all crafty things. She's a huge fan of *Star Trek*, along with other geeky things, like *Star Wars*, *Batman*, *MacGyver*, *The Hitchhiker's Guide to the Galaxy*, *Harry Potter*, and *Lord of the Rings*. As a designer, she makes whatever comes into her head.

Kirk and Picard work together to stop Tolian Soran in *Star Trek Generations.*

ABOVE: Tuvok mind-melds with Janeway in "Flashback" (*VOY*). **OPPOSITE:** An early encounter with the Borg aboard the NX-01 in "Regeneration" (*ENT*).

A recent graduate of the MA Fashion program at Ryerson University, **Ashley Lotecki** also holds a BA in design (fashion communications). Her graduate thesis focuses on cosplay and costume fandom in North America, an extremely popular activity in which individuals costume themselves as fictional characters. She currently specializes in footwear development, textile design, illustration, branding, and costume design. Ashley is also interested in sustainable clothing, experimenting with wearable technologies, and researching other areas of fandom. You can find her work online at www.thesmashworks.com.

Heather Mann is chief editor of DollarStoreCrafts.com and specializes in transforming inexpensive materials into stylish and simple craft projects. Her favorite *Star Trek* movie is *Star Trek VI: The Undiscovered Country*.

With a background in painting, drawing, and traditional sculpture, **Shove Mink** (aka Croshame) begrudgingly took up crocheting in October 2009. What was at first a tenuous relationship with the craft soon blossomed into an all-out obsession when she began making her own strangely humorous and macabre amigurumi

designs in January 2010. Originally from San Francisco, Shove currently resides with her husband, Chuck, and Pomeranian, Manson, in Denver. For more of her work, please visit www.croshame.com, www.etsy.com/shop/croshame, and www.shovemink.com.

Diana L. Payne was first introduced to *Star Trek* by the 2009 movie and left the theater totally enamored with Spock. Now she eagerly awaits her enlistment in Starfleet. Until then, she keeps herself busy doodling, crafting, and figuring out how to get her writing degree to work in a science field.

Katie Smith is a published artist currently living in Dallas/Ft. Worth. She loves scrapbooking, sewing, quilting, mixed media, and trying new craft techniques. She has been crafting and creating since she was a young girl, but started her blog, Punk Projects, in January 2010. On Punk Projects she posts craft tutorials and inspiration, and features other artists. She also loves anything *Star Trek* and loves to combine crafting and *Star Trek*. You can find her online at www .punkprojects.blogspot.com and www.etsy.com /shop/punkprojects.

Samantha Townsend is a sometimes-substitute teacher, a sometimes-work-at-home seamstress, and an always mother to one intrepid young ensign. She lives in the northeast of England and enjoys blogging about sewing and baby stuff over at http://geekysweetheart.com. She also loves karaoke, beer festivals, cheesy eighties rock music, and car boot sales. On a related note, she owns far too many dresses made out of tablecloths and curtains.

OPPOSITE: Romulan Commander Toreth aboard the warbird *Khazara* in "Face of the Enemy" (*TNG*). **ABOVE:** The *DS9* crew (left to right): (top row) Worf, Jake Sisko, Odo; (middle) Miles O'Brien, Quark, Kira Nerys; (front) Jadzia Dax, Benjamin Sisko, and Julian Bashir.

ABOUT THE AUTHOR

Angie Pedersen started on her geek path early, watching episodes of the original *Star Trek* series with her dad. While she remembers seeing *Star Wars: Episode IV* and *Star Trek II: The Wrath of Khan* in the theaters during their premiere releases, she hopes you won't do the math on that. She is actually "multicraftual"—in addition to knitting and crochet, she also enjoys scrapbooking (paper, digital, and hybrid), a little sewing, and upcycling thrift store finds into repurposed goodness. Angie is the author of three best-selling scrapbook journaling books: *The Book of Me*, *Growing Up Me*, and *The Book of Us*. You can find Angie at her blog, http://angiepedersen.typepad.com/, and on Twitter: @angiepedersen.

Spock contemplates the death of Captain Kirk while on a mission to rescue the *U.S.S. Defiant* in "The Tholian Web" (*TOS*).